The Infidel

The Infidel

PIERRE PICCARD

thistledown press

Library and Archives Canada Cataloguing in Publication

Piccard, Pierre, 1959-
The infidel / Pierre Piccard.

ISBN 1-894345-88-6

1. Armenian massacres, 1915-1923–Fiction. I. Title.

PS8581.I3317I53 2005   C813'.6   C2005-904851-4

Cover photograph by Russell Monk/Masterfile
Author photo by Jennifer Godijn
Cover and book design by Jackie Forrie
Printed in Canada

Thistledown Press Ltd.
633 Main Street, Saskatoon, Saskatchewan, S7H 0J8
www.thistledown.sk.ca

| Canada Council for the Arts | Conseil des Arts du Canada | | Canadian Heritage | Patrimoine canadien |

Thistledown Press gratefully acknowledges the financial assistance of the Canada Council for the Arts, the Saskatchewan Arts Board, and the Government of Canada through the Book Publishing Industry Development Program for its publishing program.

To Hasan, Şaban and Mohammed,
Muslims who reached out to me, a
Christian.

CONTENTS

"God is Great!"

Jesus the Infidel transformed my life. Many, including my father, say he ruined it, but I disagree. I won't deny, however, that everything is different now.

I first learned about Jesus during a Friday riot. Rioting was a seamless element of worship in those days; the *imam*'s harangue preceded ritual prayer, the riot followed it. After the final "Amen" the devout spilled from the mosque onto the vast, cobble-stoned Beyazit Square to vent their spleens. They'd be joined by angry trade unionists, embittered mothers whose sons had disappeared in custody, and disaffected students. They would wave balled fists in unison and shout *"Allahu Akbar!"*, "God is Great!", intermingled with insults and obscenities, at the ranks of riot police. When they started hurling paving stones, overturning cars and breaking windows, the police, backed by water cannon and tear gas, would charge.

Every Friday afternoon, prior to riot-time, I'd stroll to the bustling tea garden tucked into a corner of the square, in the thruway between the Grand Mosque and book market leading to the Covered Bazaar. I'd find my table and order tea from Ali, the same obsequious Ali who'd served Father when he was a student. My table protruded slightly onto the square, and was thus well situated for noting all that took place there. It was my table; I paid Ali to reserve it for me on Friday afternoons.

One such Friday, just as I found my spot, someone called my name. I turned around to see a stoop-shouldered man smiling at me over *The Morning* two or three tables away. The gangly individual came to his feet, put the newspaper under his arm, picked up his glass of tea, and approached me, baring unevenly spaced teeth.

He was about my own age. A Kurd, I determined, a vaguely familiar looking Kurd. I had seen that lean face, with its longish nose, bushy mustache and close-set eyes, before.

"Tarik Kemal!" he repeated triumphantly. He put his tea down, held out his hand and I shook it. Then he pulled up a chair uninvited, slouched into it, and gestured with his other hand, bidding me sit down. He wore a clean, carefully ironed but faded shirt, and threadbare trousers. He projected the hollow confidence of small men, I thought.

"Pleased to meet you again," I responded, trying to think where I had seen him before.

"Haven't seen you since graduation," he said.

That jogged my memory. The guy had been a year behind me. "When you started writing for *The Morning* I became your devotee!" he enthused, pompously whacking the paper with the back of his hand. "I love your take on things . . . "

I vaguely remembered he'd been something of an outsider. The pimples were gone. He seemed more at ease with himself than I remembered. He had a slightly unusual name . . . Malki, Mulki, no Melki. Melki. That was it.

"Thank you. I'm flattered." I responded. "You're Melki, right? You were a year behind me over there," I added, pointing to the Faculty of Arts on the far side of the square.

We reminisced a bit about our student days, and then brought each other up to date. After graduation he'd had a hard time finding permanent employment. He gave some private English lessons and did translation work. He looked sad as he stirred his tea.

"*Allahu Akbar!*" The *imam*'s clear voice reverberated across the square. The spill-over crowd, barefoot or wearing socks and arranged in ranks and files on cheap plastic mats before us, stood up and placed their right over their left hands. The *imam* sang the first Sura and they dropped their arms to their sides and bent forward. Melki and I sat quietly, sipping our tea and watching them pray.

"Praise to God the Greatest." The voice from the minaret rang out.

The crowd straightened and responded: "God listens to those who praise Him". The low murmur rolled across the square.

"*Allahu Akbar!*"

The crowd dropped to its knees, reverently touching foreheads to ground.

"*Allahu Akbar!*"

Suddenly Melki leaned over the table, his fists clenched before him. "We have no future here," he blurted out. "Another six weeks and I'm gone. I'm off to America. To California," he added, maliciously I thought.

"What do you mean, 'we have no future here'. My reporter's instincts suddenly came alive; I presumed he referred to The General's policy of driving the Kurds from their villages.

"I'm a Chaldean," he said with an emotional quiver in his voice

"What's that?" I sat back, genuinely interested.

"We are an ancient people." His chin jutted forward as he spoke. "We pre-date Muhammed, Jesus Christ and most of the prophets. We trace our roots back to Nebuchadnezzar and beyond."

"You may have deep roots," I said, sarcasm creeping into my voice, "but there can't be many of you around. Kurds, Turcomans, Armenians, Alawites, Yezidis, Zazas, Circassians," I numbered the names of dissident sects and minorities off my fingers, "but I've never heard of Chaldeans."

Prayers were completed. The crowd inside the mosque spilled out and joined their co-religionists on the square.

"You're right." His voice was somber. "There are only a few of us left. Four thousand years of history is coming to a close. Our people are scattered, our language, Aramaic, the language of Jesus Christ, is dying out, our churches are demolished, our culture has disappeared. There are none of us left in the East, the land of our forefathers. The civil war forced us to leave our villages for the cities, and The General's racist laws are driving us from the country altogether." He looked wistful as he sipped his glass of tea.

The riot was listless that week. A fluid wall of fundamentalists poured out of the Great Mosque's esplanade and picked up their chant. "*Allahu Akbar! Allahu Akbar! La illah illa Allah!*" "God is Great! God is Great! There is no God but God!" The cameramen got some close-ups for the evening news. The double ranks of police watched impassively, billyclubs in one hand, clear plastic shields in the other.

Melki hunched over the table again and looked at me intently. "If you want a good story," he shouted above the din, "I'll introduce you to Jesus the Infidel." His voice had that emotional tremor again. "He's an old man — God knows how old. He himself doesn't know when he was born; it was before living memory! But, judging from what he's told me, it must have been sometime between 1905 and 1908. When he left his village a couple of years ago the last Chaldean was pried from our ancient heritage. When he dies, four millennia of history ends. You should meet him. He's a great storyteller." Melki looked at me with hopeful eyes, as if he wanted to atone for his desertion by getting his people some belated publicity.

I stared at the dreary riot for a long, hard moment; it was already running out of steam.

"Chaldeans." I sipped my tea and sounded out the word. It had a deliciously historic ring to it. Chaldeans. Who had ever heard of Chaldeans? Melki had referred to churches. So they were non-Muslim, non-Turks. Little wonder The General wanted rid of them.

A tiny Christian minority with their own culture and language that nobody knew existed, of no danger to anyone, yet wiped out by a general pursuing membership to the biggest Christian club of all, the European Union. My editor might be interested in that take.

"Why not?" I said, giving in to a reporter's gut feeling.

Most leads, but not all, are dead-ends. I was prepared to give this one the benefit of the doubt. Interesting stories came from unexpected sources, and Melki had popped up from nowhere, to tell me something that might be exploited politically. It was worth an exploratory visit.

Suddenly a penny dropped, and I looked at Melki with fresh interest. This encounter, it dawned on me, was no coincidence. The man really had read my articles and knew what themes would pique my interest. I felt manipulated, yet intrigued at the same time.

We arranged to meet several days later, and shook hands. He got up and left. I thought I spotted an assertive swagger in his step.

~~~

"Who is it?" A woman's voice called from the other side of the door.

"It's Melki. Open the door, Shimone, we've come to see Jesus!"

The door opened a crack and a dark eye peered suspiciously over the security chain. The eye moved from Melki to me, and lingered there.

"Don't worry, Shimone, he's a friend. Open the door. He wants to meet Jesus."

The door closed. I heard the rattle of the security chain, and then it re-opened. We stepped into a dank, murky entryway; the darkness reduced the girl to a shadow. Melki brusquely walked passed her and led me up a rickety staircase to a dim landing, where we turned down a narrow hallway and headed for a door. He obviously knew his way around, and I wondered if he was related to these people. He rapped hard; I feared he might punch his fist through the thin plywood.

A feeble voice uttering something indistinguishable drifted through the cracked wood. Melki turned the handle and stepped inside. I followed.

I would get to know that tiny room intimately. There was a cot, neatly made, against the back wall. At its foot, to my immediate right, was another doorway. It was covered with green curtain material. At the head of the cot, which ran virtually the length of the back wall, stood a hard-backed chair with a large book lying open on it. A weary chest of drawers carrying an old-fashioned radio was pushed against the opposite wall. Squeezed at a forty-five degree angle in the far left corner, with the chest of drawers on one side and the sole window on the other side, stood an armchair with an old man in it. An abundance of red flowers bursting from a rusting paint tin sat precariously on the windowsill. To my left, across from the old man, was a threadbare couch. A shaft of light, broken here and there by the languidly nodding geraniums, created a dappled, impressionistic effect on the scant furniture and worn, brown carpet.

Melki moved toward the old man, bent forward, lifted a quivering hand, kissed it and, as a gesture of respect, pressed it to his forehead.

"How are things, Mr. Jesus?" Melki shouted. The trembling head turned first to Melki, then to me. Its cheeks were sunken, the skin papery, the lips thin, the nose large and mottled, the eyes shielded by thick-lensed glasses. Scotch tape held one of the glasses' arms to the rest of the frame. A whispy tuft of white hair, which the breeze from the window was teasing, decorated the blotched skull. A grey blanket lay across skinny legs, and a blue shirt buttoned to the collar covered a sunken chest and narrow shoulders.

"I brought a friend!" Melki said loudly, pointing in my direction.

I moved from the entrance and shook the old man's trembling hand. It was heavily veined, brittle, dry. I could have crushed the feather-light bones with little effort.

The man looked at me through his thick lenses, and I thought I spotted a glimmer of intelligence in the enlarged coal-black eyes. He nodded toward the couch.

"Sit down, sit down. Don't just stand there, make yourselves comfortable." His voice was feeble and marked with the heavy, guttural accent of the East. "Melki, it's been a while. I hear you're off to America." I followed Melki to the couch.

"Yes, Mr. Jesus!" Melki nodded. An awkward moment followed. I sensed the old man's disapproval.

"How is your arthritis?" Melki asked, seeking to break the spell.

"Not too bad. The sunshine helps." He turned his shaking head to me. "Who is your friend?" Though feeble, the voice was friendly.

"That's my friend Tarik. We studied at the university together. He wanted to meet you!"

The old man nodded. "Welcome to our house," he said. "Are you also a language teacher, like Melki?"

"No, he's a journalist!"

"Which paper do you work for?" The man pushed his wrinkled, leathery neck forward to hear better, projecting his head well beyond his shoulders. He reminded me of a turtle jutting its head from its shell.

"*The Morning*!" Melki responded. The reply was followed by another silent spell. The man pulled his head back and seemed to be thinking about something. I wondered if he disapproved of *The Morning*. Maybe he wasn't even literate, though the book on the chair suggested he might be.

The silence was interrupted by the sound of rustling coming from the green curtain. The girl who had opened the front door to let us in entered the room. I hid my surprise with difficulty. The suspicious eye and the self-effacing shadow was a well-formed girl dressed in the multi-layered, multi-coloured manner typical of Easterners, yet rarely seen in the city. She was carrying a tray with curvaceous tea-glasses. She walked past us, stooped, and with one hand pulled a collapsible coffee table from between the couch and the wall. I caught the profile of her breasts against the invading shaft of light.

As she placed the tray on the little table I noticed a Christian cross tattooed on the inside of her wrists. She disappeared into the kitchenette, to re-appear a moment later with a double teapot. She put the pot on the tray beside the glasses, knelt beside the table and looked directly at me, in a manner most untypical for village women.

"Strong or weak?" she asked. Her voice was soft, mellow, musical, though with the old man's guttural accent. Strands of unruly hair escaping the stricture of the red shawl framed her face. Her skin was light and unblemished. The large, round, piercing eyes were black as coal; I detected harshness in them.

"Strong or weak?" she repeated, raising her eyebrows.

"Weak, please." She was beautiful. I couldn't help staring at her, though in our culture that is considered rude, and might be misinterpreted.

"Sugar?"

"Two."

She dropped the cubes into the glass, stirred it and handed it to me. She had a poise and self-awareness unusual for the normally fawning, sycophantic villagers.

Although she was conscious of my gaze, she wasn't flustered and didn't blush.

I wondered if she lived with the old man. He'd said, "our house", indicating he didn't live alone. If so, where in that tiny room did she sleep? Possibly on the couch I was sitting on.

"Jesus, Mr. Tarik wants to write about Chaldeans. That's why I brought him. I thought you might be able to tell him something of your life."

Melki's sudden, loud utterance jolted me, and I reluctantly shifted my attention back to the old man. He leaned forward to hear better, maintaining his position as he concentrated his gaze on me. A whimsical smile lifted the corners of his mouth. There was something indefinably attractive about him, I thought. A mischievous glitter seemed to play in those two magnified eyes. Melki could be right; this Jesus and his Christian *houri* might conceal a story worth publishing.

CASSETTE #1, SIDE A:
JESUS' FIRST MEMORY

I normally interview known personalities in politics or the world of culture by confronting them with pertinent — and sometimes hard-hitting — questions based on earlier research. With Jesus I had to follow a different procedure, for I knew nothing about him. Initially I just wanted to get him talking, to get him on a verbal roll in the hope that, later, after I'd learned something about him and won his trust, I'd be able to pose questions leading to the kind of information I was really after, stuff which would incriminate The General. I wondered how difficult it would be to get him going such villagers as had crossed my path in the market or on the ferryboat were not loquacious, at least not with me.

It took a little while for Jesus to loosen up, but then that is true for most people. Virtually everyone is initially self-conscious when they are being recorded, and Jesus was no exception. I remember showing him the dictaphone. He scrutinized it closely, and asked how it worked. He turned it on and off, coughed into it, and had me play that back. He smiled, took it from me, pressed the Record button and started humming, then singing, something in a language I didn't know. Suddenly his wavering voice stopped, in mid-sentence it seemed to me, and he asked if he could listen to it. When he heard himself singing his face was wreathed in a beatific smile. I still have that recording; I learned later that it was the Lord's Prayer in Aramaic.

Jesus eventually placed the Dictaphone on the table, looked at me inquiringly and asked me what I wanted to know.

"Mr. Jesus, why don't you begin by telling me about your childhood?" I suggested. "Tell me about your family, your parents, your home village, your earliest memories."

Jesus turned away and stared out the window, sadness clouding his face. For a moment I wondered if I was wasting my time, that I'd touched on some raw nerve already, and wouldn't get the old codger to talk at all. I need not have worried. He turned his head back to me and began speaking.

∿∿∿

"I remember freezing in midstep. The sheep were restless, but I ignored them. I held my breath, listened carefully, then heard it again. There were gunshots, closer this time, accompanied by confused shouting echoing faintly through the valley. The disturbed flock began scattering stupidly, but I had no time for them. I pushed through the brush up to the goat trail, ran at breakneck speed, and then crawled through a thicket to the edge of a rock. From there I could look down on the village.

"Soldiers, dressed in dull green uniforms with large red epaulets and dark-brown, rectangular headgear, were breaking down doors, dragging my people from the houses, and making them stand in a long, thin column. I could see my father, my older brother, my twin brother, my little sister, my older sister, my uncles, aunts, cousins, friends, their parents — the whole village — lined up in front of the church. I saw a soldier with golden epaulets enter our home. I stared at the door leading into our house, then cringed when I heard a piercing scream. It was followed by silence, then another scream, then more silence. I saw the soldier reappear, dragging my little sister from the house. The man dropped her. She fell, and lay immobile in the dirt. Then a third scream, yet more ear piercing than the first two, split the air. A second soldier pulled my mother out of the house by her long hair. His tunic was unbuttoned. Mother stumbled behind the soldier, her face crooked toward the ground. Then, as if on impulse, the man lifted his rifle and placed the barrel against her chest. A short bark reverberated across the valley as she fell to the ground, twitched briefly, then lay crumpled up beside my sister. Mother's head was twisted in an unnatural angle, her black hair spread out, like a fan. It was the first time I had seen my mother's tresses, and the sight of them shocked me.

"A man in the column screamed and lunged forward. The soldier with the golden epaulets lifted his rifle and shot again. My father stumbled, fell, jerked on the ground for some moments, and then lay still. The crack echoed back and forth. The soldier pulled back the rifle bolt and the sun caught the glint of a cartridge shell sailing in a wide arc through the air. The man looked around, and seemed satisfied with his work.

"*İleri marş!*"he shouted in Turkish. "Forward, march!' The column shuffled forward. I watched it inch ahead and saw the cursing soldiers prodding my people with their bayonets. I could see my twin brother clinging to my uncle's arm and the dazed look on my aunt's face as she glanced back at the village. The column eventually disappeared, the soldiers' shouting got less and less until everything was silent again.

"I lay in the bushes and stared mutely, without really understanding, at the bodies of my father, mother and little sister. Then a movement caught my eye. The neighbour's dog, a mangy, brown mutt, strolled from the stable, wandered to my sister and began to lick blood off her face. A wave of revulsion welled up in me. I had to suppress the urge to vomit. I jumped from my hiding place, ran down the hill and chased the cur away. I remember looking around me in a panic of bewilderment and fright after that, then falling on my mother and crying great sobs that tore my heart from my chest. Eventually the sobbing subsided and I wept more quietly. When I could weep no more I lay still . . . "

Jesus voice trailed off. He looked down, shielding his eyes with his hands. I could see his upper lip trembling. Snot started dribbling from the large, blotchy nose, and I wondered if he could continue the narrative. Then he looked up, took off his glasses, wiped his eyes with balled fists, sucked in the mucous and smiled wanly.

"Forgive me," he said. His voice was shaky. He took a deep breath and put the glasses back on. When he started speaking again he did so firmly.

"Many hours later I woke up. I was warm and snug and comfortable. I remember thinking I'd had a horrible dream. I opened my eyes, fearful, yet curious, and looked around. Everything was different — maybe that's why I remember the details so clearly, or maybe I remember because that room would become so familiar.

I was lying under a quilt on a mattress on the floor of a hut. Above me seven old rafters supported the hard-packed dirt ceiling. A cracked window let light into the room. An old, yellowing portrait of a heavily mustached, stern-looking man wearing a fez hung crookedly on the opposite wall. Underneath the picture two ashtrays and a kerosene lamp filled a cubbyhole. There was a bronze water pot. There was no door, but an opening seemed to lead to a second room. A rush mat lay in the opening. There was also a *kilim,* and on the *kilim* a low divan with some pillows on it. The pillows were embroidered with elaborate figures of deer and birds. A walnut chest, with a rusty lock hanging from it, stood beside the divan. It had a copper tray and several small coffee cups on it. The little cups had golden edges and were painted with a regular, curvy pattern. They had little engraved handles.

"A pile of firewood lay neatly stacked in the far corner. Beside the woodpile an old three-legged, sheet-iron stove burned red hot. A tin-plated kettle was boiling on it, the water bubbling away happily, puffs of steam escaping from the snout. The chimney pipe was strung across the length of the room and disappeared into a hole in the opposite wall. It was suspended from the ceiling by pieces of wire, and had clothes hanging from it. I started hearing voices.

"'They must have taken them by surprise — there was no sign of resistance. Nine were killed and the rest marched off. We dug a big hole and buried the dead, God have mercy on them, looked for valuables, and rounded up the sheep and cattle.'

"I wondered who the voices belonged to and what they were talking about. They were speaking in Kurdish, not Aramaic.

"'Abdul Kerim, where did you find the boy?' a woman asked.

"'At first I thought him gone too. He lay on top of a dead woman. When we lifted him off her he stirred. I laid him on the donkey and took him home. God would never forgive me if I had left him to perish.'

"'God have mercy on us. You did right, Abdul Kerim. But what are we to do with the little infidel?'

"The man spoke again. 'He will become our son.' His voice was gentle. The man and the woman had no children of their own, so they raised me as if I were their own son. They did not talk about my past, and I did not ask. I tried to live obediently, trying to do things the way they did them. Abdul Kerim taught me to pray their way and, one day, took me to the mosque. The *imam* had me stand in front of the congregation and say "There is no God but God and Mohammed is His Prophet," and the congregation said, "*Allahu Akbar*!".

"The empire collapsed and the republic was established in its stead. When, years later, the man from the census bureau located the village, I had become Salih Aslan, son of Abdul Kerim Aslan. Abdul Kerim was a Muslim; I was also registered as such.

∼∼∼

The tape recorder clicked off and silence filled the room. This first effort seemed to have exhausted the old man. His head lolled forward, his voice trailed off, his breathing became deeper and more regular. I nodded at Melki, picked up my tape recorder, stuffed it into my pocket, and we left quietly.

I hid my excitement from him, but even before the end of that first interview I knew that he'd had done me a great favour. Jesus' story was, indeed, worth extracting. Although he spoke with the coarse accent of the east, you could visualize the events and places he described. His sentence structure and vocabulary suggested that he was very literate. Most importantly, most extraordinarily, he was an eyewitness willing to talk about events our historiography denies.

When we were out on the street Melki looked at me with eager eyes. "Well, what do you think?" he asked eagerly.

"Like you said, he is a good story teller," I said. "I'd like to follow it up. By the way, who's the girl? Does she live with him?"

"Leave her be." His voice turned unexpectedly raw. He turned on his heel and stomped ahead of me down the hill.

The Hill

I arranged to visit Jesus every Monday afternoon. Melki accompanied me the second time as well, and then dropped out of the picture. He was too busy preparing his departure for California. One day it dawned on me that he must have left.

It took a long time to record Jesus' story. His energy was limited. After forty-five minutes or so his breathing would slow down, his head loll forward and he'd have difficulty keeping his eyes open. At that point Shimone, when she was around, would jack his sagging body upright, and I knew I was dismissed. I tried to engage her in conversation a couple of times, but she'd simply look straight through me with those beautiful, hard eyes, then nod curtly towards the door.

So, once a week, I wended my way through the warren of alleys to Jesus' house. At first I was fearful of climbing that forbidding, intimidating hill. Flashing fluorescent tubes framed the street-level windows of the buildings in the lower reaches, the area closest to the harbour, and displayed a smorgasbord of women. There was someone for every budget.

There were the blonde "Natashas", well-endowed young Slavs whom only the rich could afford. They sat daintily on barstools or in wicker chairs, drank whisky, and adjusted their makeup or painted their toenails. When an expensive, chauffeur-driven car pulled up to one of their grimy panes and a man in a costly suit and dark glasses beckoned from the back seat, they would throw on a leather coat, step into high-heeled boots, slip into the vehicle, and snuggle up to the strange male. The car would accelerate and be gone.

Flickering neon also spotlighted the cheaper African, Filipino and Thai flesh. Their bruised, coarse skin and dead eyes lured the middle class into small, seedy, mirrored rooms above their moldering casements.

The lower classes lolled in tiny, smoke-filled, back rooms on flea-ridden mattresses with diseased Turkish, Kurdish or Arab women whose families had long ago disowned them. There were also cut rate discounts, burned-out wrecks with grotesquely painted faces, with whom you could disappear briefly behind a closet-sized, curtained-off, foul-smelling space to transact your business. Those luciferous streets nearest the harbour had banished emotion to live off man's basest instinct.

A tangled web of narrow alleys, eroding lanes, dank passageways and staircases, scarred the hill rising above those desperate streets. Crumbling three and four storey buildings clung precariously to the sloping earth, their disintegrating window frames masked by discoloured curtains, their corroding balconies jutting over the streets below. Yellowing laundry, draped from sagging lines on pulleys strung high across the streets, stirred in the scarce breeze and blocked the sunlight. Gobs of electrical cables snaked willy-nilly from one building to the next, or crossed the street at odd intervals.

Even though Melki twice showed me the way, I still got lost the first couple of times I scaled that height alone. I soon discovered, however, that virtually everyone I asked knew the way to Jesus the Infidel. I was told to turn the corner when I came to a shoeshine man and to keep walking uphill, past a barber and a grocer. Just past the grocer I was to turn right until I got to the old Armenian cemetery, where I had to turn left. I was to keep walking upwards, past a garage, and would find the house I was looking for opposite a coffeehouse. Later I got to know the Gypsy shoe-shine man, as well as the Armenian barber, the Yezidi grocer, the Kurdish guard at the cemetery, the Alevi mechanic and the Arab who ran the musty coffeehouse, and the hill above the harbour ceased to intimidate me.

Although everyone on the hill seemed to know Jesus, I doubted that Jesus knew any of them. For a time I wondered why that was so, until I realized that he incarnated them all. Nobody on the hill matched The General's racist and nationalistic criteria. His Excellency had decreed that those who failed to conform were to be eliminated. Consequently, he had pried Anatolia's sects and minorities from their remote mountains, from those flumed peaks and forgotten wadis in the southeast, where they had managed to cling to their unique identities and pre-biblical languages throughout the vagaries of history. He had driven them out and cast them into a vile slum above a foul harbour. When Jesus died, The General would have succeeded in snuffing out the last remnant of one of the ancient nations that once enriched our cultural patrimony. That sordid ghetto, that kaleidoscope of ancient cultures, would have lost another battle.

I was given safe passage through those fearful streets because its people knew I wanted to publicize the plight of the Infidel. I learned later some believed their future was in my hands.

"*Yek, du, seh, char, penj, şeş, haft, haşt.* That was Kurdish, and *Şeş* was the scary one. *Bir, iki, üç, dört, beş, altı, yedi, sekiz.* That was Turkish, and in Turkish it was *Altı.* How did we used to say it? *Ha, tre, tlotho, arbgo.* What was five again? *Hamsho.* And six? *Shevgo?* Yes, *Shevgo.* Or was that seven? I always got stuck at six. What was six again? Oh yes. *Ishto.* Funny, isn't it, that I would forget *Ishto's* name, *Ishto* the scary one. *Shevgo* was seven.

"I always woke up very early because of the nightmare. I'd lie on my back on the mattress, stare at the ceiling beams and count them. *Ishto*, or *Şeş*, the scary one, was right above my head. I often talked to God about *Şeş*.

"'God Almighty, *Şeş* is in bad shape. It is badly cracked. Please don't let it break, because then the roof will fall on my head. God Almighty, when Father Abdul Kerim returns please remind him to take the roller off the roof, because its putting too much strain on *Şeş*.'

"Sometimes when I began talking to God it was as if invisible floodgates opened. I couldn't hold myself. All my hopes and fears, my deepest desires and highest aspirations would pour out:

"'God Almighty, give us this day our daily bread.'

"'God Almighty, also give us this day our daily grapes, pistachios, eggs, milk, honey, sugar, a melon . . . '

"'God Almighty, don't let Şeş break.'

"'God Almighty, please chase the scorpions away.'

"'God Almighty, don't let snakes into the house.'

Suddenly my wish list would know no end, and my silent prayers would turn brazen: 'God Almighty, take my nightmares away. God Almighty, show me where they took my uncles and aunts and brother and sisters.'

"I'd mouth my prayers soundlessly and wipe my tears quietly. I didn't want Abdul Kerim or Mother Ayshe to think I was ungrateful."

~~~

"Abdul Kerim and Mother Ayshe lived in a hamlet called Bezal, an assembly of about twenty-five houses scattered higgledy-piggledy on a rising mountainside. Each flat-roofed, adobe house boasted two rooms and a garden, where the wife grew tomatoes, melons, cucumbers, beans and onions. We said our Friday prayers in a small mosque built of alternating layers of black basalt and white sandstone. It overlooked the village from a plateau on the upper reaches.

"A stream ran through the bottom of the valley, far below. On the hills sloping up from the stream the villagers tended their wheat, barley and lentil fields, as well as the fruit trees left them by their hapless predecessors. In the spring the farmers turned over their fields with ox plows and seeded, in the summer they weeded and irrigated, and in the autumn they harvested. The landless peasants worked as woodcutters or shepherds, caring for everyone's sheep in the mountain pastures above the treeline, just below the craggy peaks.

"Bezal was a free village, meaning that the land belonged to those who worked it. Land could be bought and sold, but only to members of the tribe. This set it apart from the villages on the plains, which belonged to wealthy landowners. The plains peasants worked the land as share-croppers.

"Bezal was once an infidel village, but the infidels who used to live in the area had been killed or deported, or had fled in the 1840s, and groups of individuals and tribal sections had moved in from the oppressed plains and laid claim to the land. These new villagers jealously guarded their property and mountain pastures from the nomadic tribes, who had to pay a collective fee for passing through the territory. Their chief exacted this fee from his clansmen, and paid it to the village headman, who kept the money as a source of patronage.

"Despite this arrangement there was invariably strife when a group of nomads crossed Bezal's territory. There would be disagreements about the sum to be paid, or villagers and nomads accused each other of stealing animals, or the villagers accused the nomads of passing too slowly, so that their huge flocks consumed too much of the village's grassland or feasted on its crops. Sometimes the disputes couldn't be settled by dialogue, and that would result in armed clashes. Fellow tribesmen then rapidly re-enforced both sides. After a couple of days of fighting a powerful outsider — a neutral tribal chieftain, a religious leader or a Turkish military commander — would impose a truce. The truce would hold until the next passage."

∾∾∾

"Whenever one of Bezal's women got pregnant, she was referred to as 'loaded', as in 'Have you heard? Ali's wife is loaded.' The village women's bellies inflated annually, and nine months later they unloaded. If a woman unloaded less than eight or nine times she dared not call herself a woman; she was considered sterile if she unloaded less than six times, or if her stomach hadn't inflated for two of the previous three years.

"Girls were a source of shame, while boys were Pashas, princes. If a woman unloaded a girl, all her work was in vain. She'd feel short-changed. After all, any woman can give birth to a girl — what was more natural than that? Pashas, on the other hand, were victories. A retarded Pasha, or one-eyed one, or a cripple, or a humpback, was equivalent to four sound girls, while a single healthy and intelligent boy outweighed any number of girls. The greatest of fiascos was not to bear sons. If, after a girl or two, the wife still hadn't unloaded a son, a deep, absorbing melancholy settled over that household.

"As I counted the roof's supporting beams early every morning Mother Ayshe rose to say her prayers. After the statutory round of ritual actions and sacred phrases, she muttered her own personal petition: 'Oh Lord, Creator of the heavens and the earth, omnipotent one, have mercy on your servant, open her womb and grant her a son of her own, one who wasn't born an infidel, because you are great . . . '

"Sometime after they adopted me, Mother Ayshe's prayers were answered. She unloaded a healthy baby boy. She and Abdul Kerim considered him God's reward for adopting me, so they named him *Ödül*, Turkish for Reward.

"We were now six in the house: Abdul Kerim, Abdul Kerim's aged father and mother, Mother Ayshe, little Reward and I. Since Abdul Kerim wasn't home much, there were usually just the five of us.

"Although Abdul Kerim was a landless villager, he didn't tend sheep or cut firewood. He was a roving dentist, travelling from village to village pulling teeth and making dentures and golden tooth-covers.

"Having golden teeth, or having them gold-plated, was all the rage in those days. Abdul Kerim was known throughout northwest Kurdistan as Abdul the Toothdoctor. Not that he had ever gone to dentistry school. There were no schools of any sort in our area, and neither his parents, nor he, nor I received the privilege of education. When Abdul Kerim was young, when his family still lived on the plains and sharecropped for the agha, lack of work and a need for cash prompted his father to send him to town, to work as an apprentice in Mahmut Bey's dentist shop. Abdul Kerim did menial jobs, all the while carefully observing his boss at work. After several years he awarded himself a Diploma of Dentistry and hit the road. Carrying a bag full of simple tools — tweezers, pliers, some bent wires with sharpened points, a small mirror soldered to the end of a screwdriver, some clay, some plaster — he headed for the mountains to practice his newly acquired profession. Later he bought a large brown horse and, with the tools of his trade in his saddlebags, he was welcomed wherever he went. He and Mother Ayshe settled in Bezal in the 1890s.

"I was always sad when Abdul Kerim left for his journeys to the mountain villages, and would wait impatiently for his return. He could be gone for weeks, even months, but when he came back, his saddle bags contained sun-dried fruit, nuts, grapes and other goodies, and he would let me ride his big brown horse while he held Reward in his lap. For a few weeks my more modest prayers would be answered. Then he'd leave again."

~~~

"Every house in Bezal had a series of big-bellied earthenware pots that lined one wall of the house. The largest of these contained flour. Next to it stood a series of slightly smaller jars holding boiled and pounded wheat, lentils, chickpeas, dried beans and rice. There were also some much smaller vessels holding molasses, salt, cooking oil and cheese. Lastly, there were the ones Reward and I liked best, into which we dipped the most, and for which Mother Ayshe often smacked us: the raisin, dried fruit, walnut and honey jars.

"Wealth was measured by the number and size of one's containers. If they were empty, that household's situation was desperate, something reflected in Mother Ayshe's prayers. 'Oh Lord God, Great and Omnipotent One, don't let anyone's pots go empty,' she murmured whenever she dipped into one of them."

~~~

"Bezal's crows were black, but they had white wings. There were always swarms of them; you couldn't get away from the beasts. They would sit in rows on the edge of the roof, or on the branches of the sycamore tree in the courtyard, cock their heads, and look down on grandfather, grandmother, Mother Ayshe, Reward and I as we struggled for our existence.

"They were merciless creatures. You'd wake up, step outside, and they'd crowd around you crying Ka, Ka, Ka, all excited about the mischief they'd spent the night devising. If Mother Ayshe was beating apricots to pulp and spreading the mush out on the roof to dry, or picking stones from the rice or cracked wheat, the crows would sit on the edge of the roof, water running from their beaks, their eyes on fire. They would hip and hop innocently back and forth, edging closer and closer. Then, quickly, one of them would dash for an apricot or a walnut or a hazelnut, and fly off, loot in beak, some of his mates in tow. He'd reappear a few minutes later pretending that nothing had happened.

"We couldn't leave anything lying around — a piece of soap, a comb, a ring, whatever — because some crow would steal it. The beasts even pecked holes through the dirt walls in order to steal from inside the house. Once we were unaware of such a crow hole for days — it wasn't until we noticed that the onions Mother Ayshe had hung from the ceiling were gradually disappearing that we located it.

"The crows teased the dog as well. Whenever Mother Ayshe fed the dog, some crow would hip and hop right in front of its nose, practically upsetting the dish. Of course the dog didn't like that. It would look at the crow from the corner of its eye, and growl and bark, but that didn't put the crow off. It would get even closer, hopping right onto the edge of the dish. The dog wouldn't stand for that. He'd give chase, whereupon the whole murder of crows that had been waiting patiently on the roof's edge, swooped down to steal the food. The crows repeated this game over and over, because the dumb dog never caught on.

"The village boys loved to go crow hunting. They'd sneak up on the beasts and shoot them with their sling-shots. Those animals seem to possess some kind of early warning system; killing even one required great skill! Whenever we managed it, we'd hang the brute's carcass from a branch as a warning to his mates.

"The crows invariably followed me to the fields. For three seasons of the year I helped the neighbours plant, weed and reap the fields. I also helped them pluck peaches, pears, apples and apricots in their orchards. At the end of the day they'd reward me with a basket of fruit, which Mother Ayshe dried on the roof, crows permitting. Mother Ayshe always gave me a cloth bundle containing some bread and cheese for lunch. One glimpse of that bundle was enough for a platoon of the black and white ruffians to separate from the main company and, fluttering from tree-top to tree-top, pursue me to whatever field or orchard I was heading. When I got to the particular place where we were working, I'd put my bundle under a tree or string it from a branch and help the other labourers. As long as I kept an eye on my bundle the crows behaved politely, but the minute I strayed too far up or down the field they would swoop down, undo the knot and start eating!

"Once, when Abdul Kerim was home, he showed me how to stretch a piece of black string around four pegs to form a square. When I put my bundle in the centre of that square the crows left it alone. They thought it was a trap."

〜〜〜

"Mother Ayshe was good to me, and so was Abdul Kerim whenever he was home. Even after Reward was born they didn't mistreat me, for Abdul Kerim feared God. He fasted during Ramadan, said his prayers five times daily, visited the mosque on Fridays and lovingly treated his horse, his customers, his wife, Reward and me. He was a gentle man. When he was around I would go to the mosque with him, but when he was away I wouldn't go.

"The villagers called me 'Little Infidel'. They didn't think I was a real Muslim in my heart, even though I had been made to say, "There is no God but God and Mohammed is his prophet" in front of everyone. They were right. In my heart I was not a Muslim.

In my heart I kept alive the bond that tied me to my brother and sisters and uncles and aunts — all who hadn't been killed but who were marched off in that long, thin column. I repeated the Lord's Prayer, just as my mother had taught us, and just as Father Bedri used to chant it in our village church in a language, which the villagers of Bezal didn't know:

Our Father, who art in heaven.
Hallowed be Thy name,
Thy kingdom come,
Thy will be done on earth as it is in heaven.
Give us this day our daily bread,
And forgive us our debts as we also have forgiven our
debtors.
Lead us not into temptation, but deliver us from the evil one.
For yours is the kingdom, and the power and the glory
forever.
Amen."

The Lord's Prayer was my link to my past."

It was raining, one of those steady, spring drizzles which eventually penetrates the most resistant material. Shimone let me in, took my soggy coat and followed me up the stairs. I knocked on the door and entered without waiting for a reply. Jesus was too deaf to hear my polite raps.

As usual, the old man was sitting in his armchair. He was looking out the window. He appeared older and more frail than usual; I wondered if something untoward had happened. He seemed glad to see me, however. We shook hands warmly, and he asked me about myself.

Shimone, dressed in her village attire, disappeared into the kitchenette to prepare tea, biscuits and the bowl of fruit, which she served in silence. I had given up trying to engage the enigmatic girl in conversation.

If I came in the early afternoon she would still be around; she always left at around four o'clock. If I arrived after that I'd miss her but, thoughtfully, she left the bowl of fruit, two little plates and two knives on the table. No matter how long I lingered afterward, I never saw her return home.

I exchanged some small talk with Jesus as I inserted a new tape into the dictaphone. He was quite oblivious to the machine now, and picked up the narration where he had left it the previous week. *"Yek, du, seh, char, penj, şeş, haft, haşt*," he began, counting the Kurdish digits on his fingers almost before I had pressed the Record button.

～～～

"For some reason I woke up earlier than usual that day. I lay on my mattress under the heavy quilt, my hands folded across my belly, counting the supporting roof beams over my head. It was still dark, though I could see my breath rising through a shaft of pale moonlight. Suddenly there was pounding on the door. A man shouted, 'Ayshe, Ayshe! Wake up, wake up!'

"Mother Ayshe sat bolt upright in bed, disturbing Reward, who shared her mattress. He started crying.

"'Ayshe, Ayshe, hurry up!' It was Uncle Shelo. Uncle Shelo and Aunt Hatije lived next door. 'Ayshe, wake up, get out!'

"Mother Ayshe leaped out of bed with remarkable agility, grabbed her headscarf, rapidly pushed her hair into it, pushed back the deadbolt, opened the door and went outside. A blast of frigid night air rushed in, and I pulled the blanket tighter.

"*Yek, du, seh, char, penj, şeş, haft* . . . I wondered what all the excitement was about. It was warm and cozy under my quilt, and cold outside. I was in no hurry to go anywhere. Mother Ayshe dashed back into the house, snatched Reward from the mattress and gave me a kick.

"'Get up, get out!' she cried. I couldn't make any sense out of it, but she wasn't in the mood to explain what was going on. She grabbed my arm, jerked me from the bed and, pressing Reward to her breast, hauled me out the door and into the front yard.

"It was cold outside, and drizzling the kind of glistening sprinkle which washes mist and fog and dust from the atmosphere and polishes everything it strikes. There was a full moon low in the sky, below the dark rain clouds, so I could see clearly. The yard filled up with people. Beside me stood Uncle Shelo and his wife Hatije, Uncle Mehmet, his wife Kerime and their daughters Selmiye and Shukriye. Uncle Hamza arrived, and other people started showing up as well. I still couldn't figure out why everyone was agitated, cursing and groaning. I was quivering; someone threw a blanket over me.

"Uncle Shelo, with the authority of one who had plastered innumerable mud-brick houses, was talking loudly. 'I woke up early, and was in the bush doing my business, when I thought I heard a crack coming from this direction. I quickly pulled up my trousers, ran over here, looked things over and said to myself, Shelo, that roof isn't going to hold up much longer. Look,' he said, pointing with his thick finger. I looked to where he was pointing. The moonlight revealed a beam I had never seen before jutting from the adobe wall.

"'That's the main support,' Uncle Shelo explained. 'It split. When it goes, the others will follow suit.'

"Just as I had feared all along, the roof was caving in, though not because of Şeş. Mother Ayshe kept running into the house to save our belongings. She pulled out our beds and quilts, and Uncle Shelo and Uncle Mehmet dragged the walnut trousseau chest into the open. It contained Mother Ayshe's most precious possessions, including the candies that came from Amid and were reserved for special guests. They also salvaged the carpet, the picture, some pillows, the kerosene lamp, and the copper cooking pots.

"Mother Ayshe wanted to rescue the food jars, but Uncle Shelo prevented her. 'Oh no,' he said, holding her by the shoulder. 'The roof is about to go. You're not going back in there.' He made her obey him.

"The roof didn't collapse all of a sudden. Just as the first touches of grey marbled the edges of the sky on that wet, chilly autumn morning, the main beam fractured and the centre of the roof dropped a foot. There were a few minutes of silence, and then *Seh* and *Penj* broke, followed by *Yek* and *Char*. I could follow their progress, because their ends stuck through the dirt walls. When the beams gave under the weight of the collapsing roof they would shudder, crack with a loud pop, and then the ends tilted upwards slowly. *Du, Haft and Haşt* were next. *Şeş* was last. I was proud of it. The heavy roller trundled from the edge of the roof to the sunken centre and crashed through. Our house had become a pile of rubble and a column of dust.

"Mother Ayshe sat on the ground and wept, her tears and the rain mingling on her cheeks. I let go of Aunt Kerime's hand, rushed to Mother Ayshe, and buried my head in her thick calico dress, but I didn't cry. I was secretly happy, because I was safely in the courtyard and the roller wasn't going to fall on my head any more.

"All our jars were broken; we were impoverished. Although I was happy to be saved from the roller, I was also very disappointed with God. Instead of answering my prayers for grapes and pistachios, eggs and milk, honey, sugar, melons and toys, he had taken what little we had.

"Fortunately, somewhere, Abdul Kerim was carrying on the struggle for life in happy ignorance of the tragedy which had struck his family. Unlike God, Abdul Kerim never failed us.

"We moved in with Uncle Shelo and Aunt Hatije, and awaited his return."

GRANDMOTHER'S GRAVE

Bus 34C runs along the bottom of Beyazit Square, zigzags through crowded streets lined with high-rise tenement buildings, then traverses several tunnels and overpasses to merge, at long last, with the ring road. Traffic permitting, it zips along this highway for about twenty-five minutes, exits, climbs a little hillock, and pulls up to a sheet of asbestos resting on four metal posts. There the chauffeur turns off the engine and gets out to smoke a cigarette on a bench under the asbestos sheet.

I was the only passenger to ride bus 34C to the end of the line. I got off with the chauffeur, and looked around curiously. The stone wall was overgrown, the poplars taller, there was more garbage strewn about and the high rise apartments and minarets had stolen closer. The wind tugging at my clothes and rustling the dry leaves on the branches overhead carried the toneless drone of the ring road up the hill.

I walked along the wall to the portal and pushed through the protesting gate, an ostentatious affair of wrought iron hanging from gateposts connected with a brick arch. The keystone had the words "*Cennet Kapısı*", "Heaven's Gate", chiseled into it. I sauntered among the haphazard jumble of headstones, looking here and there, until I found a small slab of concrete concealed in a clump of weeds. I doubted if anyone had visited Grandmother's grave since we'd discreetly interred her there twelve years earlier.

A stab of shame enflamed me. We'd been relieved to return her to the earth; that wasn't right. After consigning her to the grave we'd put her out of our minds; that wasn't right either. Little wonder Father and I led a lonely existence. No one who treats his parents thus deserves better.

I started tearing the weeds from the shallow mound. It was hard work. Time had allowed the stubborn scrubs to develop sprangling roots and a spiky bark. I began to sweat, took off my windbreaker, and continued yanking the obstinate plants from the rocky soil. The bus came to life; I straightened up, watched it do a U-turn, and listened to it rumble down the hill, back to the city. I was left with the dead.

I resumed pulling and digging until I'd cleared the resilient shrubbery from the grave. I then collected boulders from the ditch outside the cemetery. I hauled the rough chunks of granite to the gravesite, and shaped them into a cross. The vertical bar ran down the centre of the rise, the horizontal one where I imagined her chest to be. When I finished the job I slumped against a sycamore tree, and put my head between my hands. I was tired, sore and dirty, my palms and fingers raw, yet the effort hadn't succeeded in assuaging my conscience. I pulled a notepad from my pocket and copied the words Father had daubed perfunctorily onto the concrete slab more than a decade ago. The paint was drained of colour, the letters barely legible.

The following morning I phoned an old man I dared contact only in exceptional circumstances. He was the director of archives, the individual who retrieved and filed folders into and from the endless rows of bulging cabinets in the musty, cavernous basement of Police Headquarters.

Although computers had penetrated the upper floors of the forbidding security building many years ago, the amount of information its basement contained was so vast and so varied that it would have taken years to digitize. Furthermore, the process of digitizing this mass of sensitive information would have unearthed so much unpublishable information on our odious elite, that The General's bureaucracy preferred the old system. Thus, in time honoured fashion, stacks of paper printouts regarding the population's private affairs travelled down the staircase, to a white-haired man's large, wooden desk.

Every morning the man arrived at work at 8:30 sharp. A guard opened the gate for him with a polite nod. He'd cross the courtyard, pass through the front door, turn right, walk to the end of the hallway, descend a cold, concrete staircase with a well-worn wooden banister, turn left and enter a domain only he understood. He'd pull up the chair behind his large wooden desk, crack his knuckles, and start perusing the mound of incoming requests. He'd tell one of his three underlings which dossiers they were to extract from which cabinets, and to which upstairs office they were to be delivered. The old man himself filed all incoming information. Since no one else knew — or was permitted to learn — how his filing system worked, most people were kept reasonably safe from The General's excesses.

Very few journalists knew that the old man sometimes leaked information on subjects he felt strongly about, a service he provided gratis. That was his little contribution in the war against The General. He got back to me one evening later in the week and confirmed my fantastic suspicion.

The following day I headed for the university library. I had to get permission from the head librarian to access the archives I sought. The man remembered me, and had even read some of my articles. I told him I was doing a series on Enver Pasha, the strongman who had dragged our empire into the First World War, and he signed the appropriate forms. It took all that weekend, but late on Monday morning I discovered what I was looking for. It was time to pay Jesus another visit.

CASSETTE #4, SIDE A:
JESUS BECOMES ABDUL KERIM'S APPRENTICE

I had other business to attend to one of the afternoons we'd scheduled for interviews, so I arranged with Jesus that I'd come that morning. I arrived early and knocked on the door, expecting Shimone to let me in. No one opened, so I thumped it harder, but to no avail. I wondered if they were still asleep upstairs. I pounded really hard and some moments later heard Jesus' voice coming from above.

"Ya Tarik!" His head, framed in red geraniums, hung out the window. "Here, I'll drop down a key and you can let yourself in."

I let myself in, wondering what had become of Shimone.

Jesus greeted me affably, and I was glad to see him. I could not help but see him in a different light since my research. I just needed one more confirmation . . .

"Is Shimone not around?" I asked casually.

"She will show up later in the morning to make my breakfast," he replied.

"Oh, I thought she lived here!" I said surprised.

"She does," he replied. "She has finally made some friends in recent weeks and now she often spends the night with them. I'm thankful," he continued, "that there is more to her life now than taking care of an old man."

I nodded, wondering briefly about the aloof girl's friends. I pulled out the recorder and Jesus began.

～～～

"We lived with Uncle Shelo and Aunt Hatije until Abdul Kerim showed up several weeks later. When he did, he and I repaired our house together. First we built up the broken walls with rocks and freshly mixed mud. Then we chopped down four poplar trees from the stand down by the brook, and split them down the middle with wedges and a sledge-hammer. Abdul Kerim's big horse hauled the trunks up to the house, and we hoisted them onto the walls. They served as undergirding for the new roof. We then criss-crossed layers of branches over the beams and spread a foot of freshly mixed adobe on top of the branches. After that we lifted the roller back onto the roof and dragged it over wet gumbo hauled up from the creek until there was a shiny thin layer of the stuff spread evenly over the entire surface. The sun baked it like a ceramic. It was fun working with Abdul Kerim. I did my best to please him.

"One night, not long after we'd moved back into our own house, I overheard Abdul Kerim talking to Mother Ayshe. 'The boy is growing up,' he was saying. 'He is a good worker. I am going to take him along. He will be my apprentice. You will have one less mouth to feed, while he learns a useful skill. Also, the village will be glad to see him go. They believe the house collapsed because of the boy. They do not think he is a true Muslim, that, in his heart, he remains an infidel. They are afraid he will bring the Evil Eye upon the whole village.'

"'As God wills, Abdul Kerim . . . ' There was a moment's silence.

"'Do you think he is still an infidel, Abdul Kerim?' Mother Ayshe's voice had a tremor.

"'Only God knows the heart of man,' her husband replied slowly.

"If there were more words, I didn't hear them. Waves of happiness swept over me. I lay awake dreaming of the places Abdul Kerim and I would visit, of the adventures we would share and maybe, just maybe, I'd find my brothers and my sister and my uncles and my aunts . . . That night I repeated the Lord's Prayer over and over, and God felt close and caring.

"Early one morning, a day or two later, Abdul Kerim saddled his big horse and left. I wondered if he'd changed his mind. I remember being very sad that day, but toward evening he reappeared with a lovely little chestnut-coloured donkey strolling behind his big brown sorrel. The donkey made a funny braying noise when she saw me, then trotted daintily in my direction. I put my arm around her head and she laid her velvet nose on my shoulder and licked my ear. Mother Ayshe turned an old blanket into saddlebags and Abdul Kerim cut strips of leather into a bridle.

"One April dawn Abdul Kerim and I rode off. My insides were churning; I was full of mixed emotions. I looked back at the house Abdul Kerim and I had rebuilt. Mother Ayshe and Grandma stood by the gate; Reward clung to his mother's thick skirts. Further up the hill, past the twisted shapes of the cherry, apricot and peach trees, grey-black smoke billowed from Uncle Shelo's chimney. Behind Uncle Shelo's house lay the rest of the village. The piebald mosque towered over all. Bezal had been home since the nightmare; I felt a pang of longing at leaving it, even if the village thought of me as an infidel. But the thrill of adventure also surged through my body and I turned my eyes to the road ahead, to the pleated hills and ragged mountains that rose up against the pink sky."

~~~

At this point the cassette recorded the creaking sound of the door opening and closing, followed by Jesus' voice: "Welcome back, girl! Did you have a good time with your friends?"

I remember being irritated by the interruption, for Jesus had been carried away, had become almost lyrical, as he described that amazing day in his life. I wondered if he would get back into the groove, or if I'd lost him for that session.

Shimone: "I did, thank you. Have you had any breakfast yet?"

Jesus: "I had some of the fruit you left on the table, and managed to pour myself some milk."

Shimone: "I'll boil you an egg"

Jesus: "Egg? How nice! Where did you get those?"

Shimone: "My friends gave me a couple. They send their greetings to you."

Jesus: "You must have them over for a visit sometime. I'd love to meet them. The days can be long . . . No, I'm not too hungry. Let's save the egg for lunch. That will be nice . . . "

The tape then recorded some background shuffling noises, and then Jesus' voice, loud, clear and focused.

~~~

"Umm, yes, I was telling you about our departure from Bezal. We headed eastward, toward the snow-peaked smoky-grey ridges of the jumbled Zagros. Behind us the large, lonely, inverted funnel of Mount Judy rose in all her lonely splendour. To the north and south the creased green and brown foothills tapered gradually into the valley which sustained our village, and through which the scintillating stream flowed wild and free until it merged somewhere far away with the distant Zap. All around us were the mountains that had circumscribed my world. Even before the nightmare, mountains had bound my existence. Before the nightmare I'd thought that those mountains rimmed the world, that there was nothing beyond them; after the nightmare I realized that the world beyond contained much evil. Fear tempered the thrill of adventure, while, all the while, I nurtured the hope that I might, one day, be reunited with my family, and I mumbled the Aramaic Lord's Prayer under my breath.

"We rode all that day. By noon we reached the point where the road crested the first mountain pass. In the past Abdul Kerim had warned me against crossing the pass, so it was with some curiosity that I moved ahead. The valley before us was hemmed by rolling hills, purple in the distance, behind which lay a saw-tooth line of snowy peaks. The road below zigzagged sharply. No shrubs grew on the bald pass. Neither man nor animal moved up or down the steep slopes; there weren't even any crows to bring life to the quiet world below. My eyes passed lightly over the jumbled heaps of green shades to the flat and shimmering valley floor, and rested on a hamlet. It looked familiar . . .

"All at once I jolted. The place matched that of my nightmares, except that in my dreams there was no smoke rising peacefully from the chimneys. They were of guns and soldiers, of killing and a dog licking the blood from my little sister's face, of a dirty, dismal place, a place of death and violence.

"'Are you afraid, boy?'" Abdul Kerim asked kindly.

"I gazed at the peaceful village below me and more and more details of my past life came back. A thin column of smoke rose from the chimney of our house, and it was everything I could do to keep myself from running down that hill and into my mother's arms. The well was exactly where it was supposed to be, and so were the orchards, the fields and the church. Everything was carefully tended. The church looked different; then I noticed the stubby minaret pasted onto its roof.

There, in the courtyard before the church, my older brother, my twin brother, my uncles, aunts, cousins, friends and their parents were herded together and led away. Over there was the spot where the soldier in the dull green uniform with the golden epaulets shot my sister. Another soldier had dragged my mother to that place there and shot her. Her hair had spread fan-like; I could hear the ear-splitting scream. My father had lunged forward. The soldier had lifted his rifle and shot him too, and he fell and twitched on the ground, right there. I had come to think that these things had happened in an ugly place, but it was a most beautiful setting."

～～～

Jesus' eyes grew larger than normal behind their thick lenses, yet he saw neither me nor anything else in that small room on the hill above the harbour. He was focused on a little village about two thousand kilometres distant, and nearly eighty years back in time. With spasmodic hand movements he again pointed out what had happened where, who was killed on what spot, where he had hidden, in what direction the column had disappeared. Then he fell silent. His hands dropped dead in his lap, he slumped in his chair and his head toppled forward. His breath was laboured.

I looked with amazement at the old man. He could have been a writer, I thought, a novelist. I had, until then, viewed him with the condescension of the rich toward to poor. I began to realize that there was much more to this man than there appeared to be.

Shimone rose from the hard chair and hoisted him upright. It was time for me to go, yet I needed to confirm just one thing before I went.

"Jesus!" I shouted. "Jesus! Does the name Hanbak mean anything to you?" I thought I saw Shimone jerk involuntarily, while Jesus raised his head with difficulty and stared vacantly at me with those enlarged eyes of his. I wondered if he'd heard me. Shimone indicated with an angry face and an abrupt, unmistakable gesture that the interview was over. I wasn't giving up that easily, however. "Jesus!" I repeated. "Hanbak! Who was she?" Jesus looked at me blankly, and shook his head.

"Go," Shimone hissed through clenched teeth. I looked at her. There were bags of fatigue under her eyes. I picked up the dictaphone and my coat and turned toward the door. I felt both her and Jesus' gaze boring into my back as I slipped out the door and into the hallway.

GRANDMOTHER'S STORY

My grandmother's guilt at having survived, while everyone else perished, haunted her until the day they found her frail, broken body at the bottom of the elevator shaft. I know that, because Father told me the night she died that his mother believed she'd paid too high a price for life, that she shouldn't live when other, more useful, more sensitive, more generous people than herself were killed.

Father really grieved, yet he also seemed relieved to be rid of her. When, some months later, I raised the subject of grandmother again, he brushed me off.

Father is a successful lawyer. His clients include numerous high-placed individuals in both business and government. He couldn't afford to let his mother, who, like the Ancient Mariner, had the compulsion of inflicting her story on whomever she met, talk to every visitor. He kept her locked in a cheery and comfortable room in our penthouse.

I was a young teenager when she died, old enough to remember her haunting presence. Even though Father had her room redecorated after the funeral, her specter continued to pervade the house for years afterwards.

I used to visit her now and then, but she made me uncomfortable. She always sat in an overstuffed armchair, her precious Holy Book open in her lap, rocking forward and backwards like the demented person she was. Once, when Father tried to take the book away from her, she flew into such a rage that she nearly scratched his eyes out. The book seemed to connect her to something in the distant past. Whenever I entered her room she'd smile excitedly, rock violently, and unleash a compulsive stream of words.

"Tarik, stand near me and let me tell you something and never forget what I'm about to tell you. Tarik, you must never trust a Muslim. They are instruments of the Angel of Death. They killed my mummy and my daddy, the twins, and everyone else. They didn't kill my body because it was young and pretty, but they killed my soul." At first her words were slurred because no one other than Father and I ever visited her — or even knew of her existence — and because Turkish was not her mother tongue. By and by, however, her sentences would flow, though retaining their eastern accent. It was always the same story.

"Your grandfather took me and raped me and I tried to please him to save my body. He was pleased and he took me to a mosque where they put a white veil over my head and where the *imam* made me repeat 'There is No God but God and Muhammed is His Prophet'. Then they told me I was a Muslim, but I didn't want to be a Muslim. I hated your grandfather for what he had done to me, but I hid my hatred because they would kill anyone who wanted to stop being a Muslim, even if you never wanted to be a Muslim. Remember, little Tarik, they are the Angels of Death who kill both body and soul. They killed my soul and let my body live, when it would have been better for my body to die so that my soul could live . . . "

As she told her story she would look at me with empty, glazed eyes while she rocked, and her fingers would move with incessant, nervous energy.

"I had a baby and I loved my baby and I didn't want my baby to be a Muslim, for they are the Angels of Death. One day I entered the church and stole a Holy Book, and hid it in different places. When your grandfather was away and no one else was around I'd place the Holy Book in my baby's cot so he wouldn't grow up to be a Muslim. But they found the Book in my baby's cot and they beat me and they told me I was an infidel and that I wasn't fit to be the mother of a Muslim and that I deserved to die. They tore up my Book and threw the pieces into the fire, and they locked me in a little room. I never saw my baby again, although I could hear him from time to time through the wall. They wouldn't let me take care of my baby and they made my baby into a Muslim. Then baby grew up and left the house and he was gone. I wished I had died with mummy and daddy and the twins and everyone else and never had a baby, because they made my baby into a Muslim and Muslims are the Angels of Death!

"Then your great-grandfather died and your grandfather didn't want me anymore. Someone drove me to a strange city and left me on the street. I don't remember what happened after that, but when my baby found me I had my Holy Book again and I was happy because I wasn't a Muslim anymore. My baby was driving a big black car. He washed me and we drove for a long time and he took me to this nice room and he said, 'this is your new home, Mama.'

"My baby has been good to me, even though he is a Muslim, except when he tries to take my Book away and make me a Muslim again. Don't ever trust Muslims, my little Tarik, for they are the Angels of Death . . . "

We still don't understand how she managed to get out of her room, leave the house, climb the stairs, open the steel safety hatch and throw herself into the void. The fact that she did, however, expiated my father's guilt at having kept her under lock and key those many years. When he buried her we placed the old book in the coffin with her. I rifled through it before Father gently placed it between her stiff hands. It was written in a curious angular script no one could read. I remember Father's thin smile. "She was illiterate," he said, "but she loved this book."

Cassette #4, Side B:
Travels with Abdul Kerim

I feared that I might have made myself unwelcome, so I deliberately came after four for the next interview, when I knew Shimone would be out. I did not raise the unwelcome name "Hanbak" with Jesus. I was not sure if Jesus had heard me in the first place — I hoped now he hadn't.

I gave Jesus the box of baklava I'd bought on the way over, and he opened it with childish delight. His magnified eyes shone when he saw the contents.

"Haven't tasted that in years," he exclaimed. "Go get us some forks and plates, will you, Tarik? Let's eat some of it now. Be sure to put some aside for Shimone, though. She's looking too thin these days . . . "

I got some plates and knives from the kitchenette, along with two glasses of water. We ate in comfortable silence. An emotion, a feeling I hadn't really known before invaded me. It was almost as though I was with, well, like I was with family. I shook the feeling from me, imagining what Father's reaction would be to that. When we'd eaten our share I gathered up the dishes, took them to the kitchenette and quickly washed them under the tap. I returned to the livingroom, pulled the dictaphone from my pocket and placed it on the table.

"Ready?" I asked.

"Ready," he replied, and I hit the Record button.

~~~~

"That spring and summer Abdul Kerim and I traversed Kurdistan's heights, hills and hollows, to reach its hamlets and villages. For hours we rode the trails, Abdul's big horse trudging before, my chestnut donkey trotting after it.

"Day after day the sun would climb higher, its warmth giving life to the earth. The oaks, the beeches, the birches and the oleanders broke into new foliage, their fresh buds nodding in the breeze. The brooks, recently released from winter's icy grip, rushed over and around smooth, sparkling boulders, racing to the valley bottoms to form streams which, in turn, twisted and turned until they became one with the Zap. Sometimes deer leaped across the path, and sometimes the underbrush moved restlessly when a skunk or a wild boar stepped aside to let us pass.

"We stopped periodically at some spring or creek, slipped the bridles from our animals, and let them graze and drink their fill. Abdul Kerim would sit down, stretch his booted legs in front of him, lean back against some tree or boulder, fold his arms over his chest, bend his head as if in prayer, and close his eyes. I'd sit on a log and, when my chestnut donkey had drunk her fill, she would sidle up to me and I would stroke her soft, responsive nose. The big brown horse would eat for a while, then stand at rest, her head sagging, and her tail drooping. Eventually Abdul Kerim would get up groggily, tighten the saddle girth, mount, and we would continue through the unfolding green stillness.

"In the course of time the path would widen and ruts would appear. Soon fields and pastures began pushing the scrubby forest back, and we might overtake a group of peasants on their way home. The road would crest, and another village would welcome us.

"You could smell the villages from afar. In those days houses didn't have toilets. The men would rise before dark, and go to the edge of the creek or the river to do their business in happy unison. The women squatted behind the barns, where their excrement would mix with that of the animals. The kids defecated wherever they stood, wiping themselves with whatever stone or leaf lay close at hand. Every so often the women would collect the mixture of human and animal excrement from along the river and from behind the barn, water it down to liquid mash, and then mix straw into it by trampling it with their feet. The stench accompanying this task could be smelled from one end of the valley to the other. But village women were tough. With watering eyes and burning cheeks they'd force the mash into wooden forms, which they laid in the sun to dry. The effort of making these cakes, which burned like peat, turned the women's eyes into pools of blood. Trachoma blinded many of them

"Travellers were always welcome in those remote areas. The village head would either accommodate us in his home or let us stay in the special shack he kept for the few itinerants who pushed that deep into the mountain masses. The horse and donkey were put out to pasture, and no payment was thought of except Abdul Kerim's tales.

"News from the outside world was hard to come by, so for the first couple of days all our meals would be with the village head. Abdul Kerim's function as a conduit of news to distant villages was as much appreciated as his dental skills. He freely shared what he'd picked up from other travellers and gleaned from outdated newspapers and journals left in the inns and coffeehouses of distant towns:

"'Enver Pasha has fled to Russia . . . The Greeks broke through in Eskishehir . . . Ismet Pasha's troops held their ground at the village of Inonu . . . Parliament gave General Mustafa Kemal dictatorial powers for three months . . . The lines around Ankara held . . . The Greeks were routed . . . Smyrna was burned to the ground . . . The French took Edessa and are moving toward Iconium . . . The British have seized Istanbul . . . General Mustafa Kemal's troops were pushing towards Istanbul . . . General Mustafa Kemal signed a peace treaty with the Bolsheviks and secured the eastern front . . . General Mustafa Kemal confronted the British at Chanakkale and the British turned tail. Long live General Mustafa Kemal! Marshal Mustafa Kemal abrogated the treaty of Sevres. Long live Marshal Mustafa Kemal! The Sultan escaped to Europe and the empire has collapsed . . . Marshal Mustafa Kemal has established a Turkish Republic and signed a treaty with the European powers in Lausanne. Where is Lausanne? Who cares! Long live President Mustafa Kemal! No, there was no mention of a Kurdish state, as there had been in the treaty of Sevres, but the French have left for good. As a gesture of good will they gave us Arab Hatay, including the harbour of Alexandretta. Long live the French! Long live President Mustafa Kemal!'

"The villages Abdul Kerim and I visited that spring were cut off from the rest of the world during the long winter months, and their people were news-starved. There would be a hubbub of voices as people digested what they heard. Oil lamps and candles would flicker as women lugged large trays with rice, mutton and yogurt into the room, and the din would subside as people took up their position around the trays and tucked into the food. Abdul Kerim was always given the place of honour, on the cushion away from the door, but he'd insist I be allowed to eat with the men, though from the far end of the tray, from the place closest to the door. After the meal the men reclined against long, rectangular cushions, poured numerous glasses of tea through lumps of rock sugar held between their teeth and lower lip, and analyzed the new information, trying to figure out how it would affect them.

"We'd stay in any one village from a couple of days to a week, depending on the amount of work there was. In the mornings, Abdul Kerim would wait beside the mosque entrance. Before long the day's first customer, some agonized soul with a rag tied around an inflamed cheek, would show up. Abdul would seat the distressed individual on a borrowed stool and have him or her tip their head back and open their mouth wide. He then examined each tooth with the screwdriver to which he had soldered a highly polished piece of metal. Then, using one of several wire instruments he had manufactured, he would tap and poke each tooth to determine which ones were the offenders.

"Throngs of curious children along with a knot of gaping adults inevitably gathered to witness Abdul the Toothdoctor at work. They would stir with the restless excitement of a crowd witnessing an execution as Abdul examined his hapless victims. Nevertheless, Abdul Kerim was nearly as popular in his capacity as a dentist as he was as a conduit of news. This was due to the satchel of homemade brown powder he carried with him. Before he started jerking rotting teeth out of jaws, he poured some of this powder on a leaf and made his patient snuff it up his or her nostrils. This powder caused the individual to relax almost instantly. Abdul Kerim manufactured the stuff by squeezing the milky substance from the seedpods of the little poppies with the pretty white and red flowers that grew on certain mountain pastures, and letting it dry in the sun. It was a very effective pain reliever.

"After the powder took effect, Abdul Kerim would reach for a pair of pliers, insert it into his patient's mouth, grab the guilty tooth and wrench it this way and that. You could hear a series of audible cracks and fractures as he worked it, and the victim would scream in spite of the dose of opium he had just snorted. Then, with a final twist, Abdul would rip the offending member from the jaw and, with a flourish, hand it to his long-suffering patient as a memento. The relief that people experienced after their ordeal was usually so instant and so complete that they gladly paid Abdul Kerim his due. Abdul Kerim didn't charge a set fee for pullings; everyone simply paid what they could afford.

"It was Abdul's skill in making golden teeth that eclipsed even his 'opium assisted' extraction abilities. Golden teeth were all the rage with both sexes in those days. Women would have healthy teeth pulled just so Abdul the Toothdoctor could insert one of his golden replacements. Although Abdul had devised a way to cover healthy teeth with a golden cap that cost less and was a lot less painful to install, it had an irritating tendency to drop off, and was considered a poor substitute for his solid gold productions.

"After pulling the tooth, Abdul made his customer draw their lips as far back as they could, shoved the lump of clay he carried in his saddle-bag into the patient's mouth, and made him or her bite into it. Pouring some lime mortar into this clay mold then gave him a replica of the customer's mouth. Using more lime mortar, he then created a model tooth that filled the gap in the replica. He would push this lime tooth into another piece of clay to make another little mold, spread a wire across the mold and pour some melted gold alloy into it. The metal would set rapidly, and when the result was removed from the clay encasing, Abdul had a golden tooth — or set of teeth — with a wire protruding from either end. Using the replica of the customer's mouth he would bend and twist the wires so they clamped nicely onto the remaining teeth. A final buffing, and the job was done.

"My responsibilities as Abdul Kerim's apprentice grew with time. At first I was merely called upon to hold the heads of frightened customers steady by putting my right arm around the backs of their necks and pressing their foreheads down with my left hand. I could soon anticipate what tool Abdul needed next and would hand it to him without any exchange of words taking place. Later I learned to mix the lime mixture for the mold and melt the gold alloy."

At this point a nearby mosque sounded the mid-afternoon call to prayer. Deaf as he was, Jesus was oblivious to the noise outside and kept on talking. When the recording picked him up again, he had changed subjects.

"Together we travelled through wide, fertile valleys, forded violent rivers, climbed narrow mountain passes and visited numerous villages. Sometimes, when we didn't achieve our objective, we would spend the night in the open. Believe me, lying with your head on your saddle blanket, gazing at the twinkling stars on a warm summer night is one thing, sitting out a spring storm is quite another. Cold and soaked to the bone, we would seek shelter from some ledge or tree or bush, and hold the horse and donkey by their bridles, in case lightening and thunder frightened them and caused them to flee.

"Sometimes shepherds would share their hut or cave with us. The shepherds would listen to Abdul Kerim for hours without confirming or denying anything they heard. When they did speak it was of how they led their sheep for weeks at a time from one mountain pasture to the next. In simple language they would tell of their adventures: of how they stayed awake on moonless and foggy nights to protect their flock from the sneak attacks of wolves, of how they slept in the mouth of the caves they drove their sheep into, of how they herded their flocks to whatever warmth or shade they could find. They knew every rock and boulder, every razed fortress and castle, every spring and creek in the surrounding mountains and valleys. They possessed no land, trod barefoot over the mountains and didn't know the meaning of the words 'flu' or 'cold'. They were humble men whose presence was a source of strength and comfort to the vulnerable creatures in their charge. They reminded me of those times before the nightmare when I was allowed to take our family's sheep up to the pastures near our village . . .

"Sometimes our objective was a town. I loved the towns. We always stayed in inns, those warm and friendly places built around cobblestone courtyards. Abdul Kerim never pulled teeth in towns, because there were other tooth doctors there, tooth doctors with real diplomas. We would spend two or three nights so that Abdul Kerim could get caught up on the news. Although he had never been to school, he had somehow learned both the obsolete Ottoman and the new Latin alphabet, and he would spend hours reading old newspapers and discussing their contents with the other itinerant traders and workers. We'd sit on little wooden stools and drink tea, while the men swapped news and told stories. In the evenings, a travelling musician might play his lute or his flute, and sing about eloping with his childhood sweetheart. An entertainer might make his shadow puppets parody the ways of sheiks and aghas. A wandering dervish might recite the love poetry of Yunus Emre or Maulana irRumi, or a ventriloquist, sitting quietly in his corner, might make the chicken roasting on the spit, or an overburdened donkey, complain bitterly about its lot in life.

"That spring and summer we crossed and criss-crossed the Zagros Mountains. Then, one day, we crested a hill, and Bezal lay on the slopes opposite us.

"Mother Ayshe hadn't changed at all, but Reward had grown considerably. Grandma had died, and lay buried on the hillock to the left of the house. We prayed over her grave. It was good to be back."

I Am Tarik Kemal

My parents are divorced. My mother, her second husband, and my two half-sisters live on the Asian side of the city, across the Bosphorus. The fight over my custody is the most vivid of my early memories. I was five, confused, and cried a great deal. I haven't cried since.

After Mother's departure, Father sent me to an English language private school. For twelve years a taxi picked me up early every morning, drove me to school and, in the late afternoon, took me home again. The school gave me as good an education as our country has to offer.

When I got home the cook, a large, jolly, buxom woman, would give me a snack and inquire about my day. I'd answer her questions, eat my fruit or cake, then go to the basketball court to shoot hoops with friends until suppertime. Homework usually kept me busy after that.

My father is very persuasive in the courtroom, but he is a taciturn man. Every evening we'd sit at opposite ends of the dining room table and eat mostly in silence. He might inquire about my day, and I'd tell him it went well. His ability to keep his mouth shut contributed as much as his courtroom manner in making him a trusted lawyer to the country's elite.

Every summer he and I took his Mercedes to the Mediterranean coast, where he has a villa. For four or five weeks I'd lounge on the beach or go hiking, fishing, or boating with local friends, while Father ran his office by telephone from the sundeck. We weren't close, but I was not uncomfortable in his presence, as most of my friends were with their fathers. He never tried to squeeze me into some preconceived mold of his and, as I grew older, I was glad he had prevailed in the battle over my custody.

There was one major difference between my basketball and "beach bum" friends, and me. They were all members of large families, of clans. Even if they had but one or two siblings, they could draw from a vast array of uncles, aunts, cousins, and other, more distant relatives. In our country the extended family provides the individual with a support network through which one's social needs are met, and within which marriages and business partnerships are arranged. I had no such network. My mother and half-sisters were strangers to me, and Father appeared to have no family of his own. I only knew that he was born in the eastern city of Diyarbakir, or Amîd as it is known to locals, and that his family there had sent him to Istanbul to study when he was a boy. I also knew he'd only been back once, to pick up his mother, upon what I presumed was his father's death.

Years ago, when I was still a youngster, I once asked Father if he had any brothers or sisters. He'd dismissed the subject with a disparaging shrug. "There may be some distant connections in the east, but I have lost track of them." I had a lonely childhood, though I was only dimly aware of it at the time.

In my last year of high school I informed Father that I wanted to major in journalism and political science. He gave me a bemused look. "Major in journalism and English instead," he suggested.

"Why?" I asked.

"In this country, political science, like history and theology, is not allowed to develop. Study those subjects later, in Europe or America, if you're still interested in them then."

I followed his advice, and when I graduated four years later I wanted to study political science in Europe or America.

"Get a year or two of work experience first."

I landed a job at *The Morning*. The pay wasn't great, but then money wasn't an issue.

My years at *The Morning* opened my eyes as nothing else could have done to the graft, patronage, nepotism and corruption that pervaded The General's government. The longer I worked for *The Morning*, the deeper my disillusionment with politics grew, and the less I wanted to study political science. I turned to investigative reporting instead. Father approved. With the help of some allusions on his part, I uncovered a number of unsavoury affairs, including an insider-trading scandal and the fact that the city's deputy police chief had regular liaisons with a stunning Circassian woman, who was also the mistress of a Mafia boss.

～～～

The housekeeper had put the supper dishes into the dishwasher and left. Bartok drifted from the CD player. A fire crackled in the fireplace. I was glancing through *The Nationalist*, *The Morning*'s archrival. Father was typing something into his laptop.

"I visited Grandmother's grave the other day," I said.

"May God have mercy on her," he said, and continued typing.

"It was overgrown with weeds. I cleaned it up."

"That was kind." He glanced at me briefly and continued typing. "Are you pursuing some kind of journalistic hunch?" I wondered whether the question was sarcasm or an invitation to pursue the subject. It didn't matter.

"Yes I am. I'm investigating you."

This time he looked up and smiled. He then folded the computer screen down, placed his elbows on the table and rested his chin on clasped fingers.

"What have you discovered?"

"Using boulders, I fashioned a Christian cross on her grave."

"You knew she was a Christian. What else have you discovered?

"I was hoping you would help me. You see, I am actually investigating both of us," I replied. "Who are you? Who am I?"

"You don't want to know," he said curtly. He stood up, picked up his computer and left for his room. I stared at his back as he walked down the hall. If he thinks he can dismiss me as easily as that, I thought, he underestimates me.

Jesus' narrative turned into more than the autobiography of an eloquent old man; it became an eyewitness account of those formative events which took place during the first quarter of the twentieth century, the very events which The General's historiographers had rewritten.

The General's views on the subject of the Young Turk and Kemalist Revolutions were notoriously narrow, almost as narrow as those of the population at large. And his ubiquitous police ruthlessly suppressed those who sought to evaluate that era by normal historical criteria. The official version of that period had been imposed with such thorough effectiveness, that even I did not begin to doubt it until I had known Jesus much longer, and had verified much of what he told me.

∿∿∿

"For about eight years Abdul Kerim and I criss-crossed the Zagros mountains in search of rotting teeth. During that time he taught me, in his own, informal way, everything he knew. He taught me to read the old Ottoman alphabet, as well as the new Latin one, by forming the letters in sand, or by using his spittle on hard surfaces. Together we devoured a thousand old newspapers in a hundred inns and teahouses, and compared their contents with the gossip we'd picked up along the way. Abdul Kerim also taught me dentistry; I became as good as he was at manufacturing raw opium, pulling teeth and making golden replacements. I also got to know the mountains, the passes and the valleys of the Zagros, and the villagers grew to appreciate me, too, though I never commanded the respect Abdul Kerim had earned.

"Mountains everywhere are seedbeds for heresies and the home of lost causes, and the mighty Zagros, bounded in the north by the towering Ararat and in the south by the Mesopotamian plateau, was no different. Since the beginning of religion, fakirs, sufis and mystics have headed for the caves in that region of snow-capped peaks. From there their teachings dribbled to the valleys and built up like the fertile sediments in which the isolated and super-stitious villagers toiled. Here the numerous cults and beliefs, which the religious elite managed to suppress on the more accessible plains, continued to flourish.

"There were Yezidi villages where they placated Malak Tawus, the Peacock Angel, their euphemism for *Şaytan*, or Satan. Some of them still exist. Their religion is centred on a tomb in northern Jezira. They draw their inspiration from their holy books, the *Kitab al Jalwah*, the *Book of Emergence*, and the *Mishaf Resh*, the *Black Book*. During their festivals they carry copper peacocks from village to village. They refuse to wear blue and won't eat lettuce, because they believe that Satan once hid in a lettuce patch. They are not allowed to urinate standing up, and speak a form of Kurdish which has excised the "sh" sound, since it forms the beginning of *Şaytan*'s name — they fear using his name in vain, even if by accident. When we were with them we would be careful not to wear anything blue, squat

71

when urinating, and would avoid the "sh" sound. Instead of "*şeş*", for instance, we'd say "*ses*".

"Then there were the villages of the Ahl-i Hakk. They believe that there are seven divine manifestations, the first of which was Khawandagar. They also held that Muhammed's cousin Ali ibn Abu Talib was one of these manifestations, and that the last one, the founder of the Ahl-i Hakk, was someone callèd Sultan Sohak. They sacrifice roosters, because the rooster symbolizes the transitional moment at daybreak, between light and darkness. Some of them are fire worshippers, like the ancient Manicheans and Zoroastrians, and some of them believe in the transmigration of souls, and in reincarnation. In the villages of the Ahl-i Hakk we were always treated with extreme respect and politeness.

"Alawite villages are different because they have no public place of worship. No minaret, no mosque. Their secret rites involve initiations into ever increasing levels of knowledge, and includes the belief that emanations of God exist in prophets, mystics and in Jesus Christ. They hold that the Milky Way is made up of the deified souls of true believers. They baptize their children and celebrate Christmas, practices they picked up from neighbouring Armenian villages.

"In the decades after the genocide the Armenian villages were sad places. Their houses and churches were in ruins. Their villages were the first to die out, for there were not enough able bodied males left to restore the wrecked terraces. Such as survived left, one family at a time, for Amîd or Istanbul.

"There were also Syriac villages. There were not many of them, but they were not as sad as the Armenian ones.

Usually their churches and terraces were still intact, and the smell of death didn't hang over them.

"One day we entered a village on the banks of the Habur River. At first glance it seemed no different from other such Syriac hamlets that had escaped the killings. The smell of death did not hang over it, the terraces and fields were cared for and the irrigation channels well preserved. The church and the houses were undamaged, well-tended horse and donkey carts bustled hither and yon, unveiled women wearing layers of colourful cloth and men wearing cummerbunds went about their business. Abdul conversed with the men in Kurdish, and had soon made arrangements for the night with one of the village elders. After welcoming us warmly the man led us down the street to his house.

"As usual, a swarm of curious kids followed Abdul and me. Suddenly my heart began to beat faster while the blood seemed to drain from my body. The kids all around me — they were chattering a different language. It wasn't Kurdish or Turkish, two languages I knew. They were yakking away in something else, yet I understood almost everything they said! I understood, but couldn't understand how that could be.

"Then, as if someone clicked a button, my brain began repeating the Lord's Prayer: "Our Father, who art in heaven, hallowed be your name. Your kingdom come, your will be done on earth as it is in heaven . . . " Lights went on in my head. The kids around me were talking my special Lord's Prayer language among themselves!

"My breath came in quick little bursts, though I tried to control myself. I didn't want Abdul to know, for I loved him and didn't want to hurt him, or worse, to lose him. He was all I had! And so I didn't let on that I understood the people. Also, even though I understood them, I couldn't talk to them, because it had been so long since I had spoken the Lord's Prayer language. I had forgotten, even though I could understand. And so I said nothing to anyone. To the villagers, as to everyone else, I was Salih, the son of the Kurd Abdul the Toothdoctor. I only spoke Kurdish with them. But when we sat in the church courtyard in the evenings and drank tea, I would strain my ears to listen to the conversations around me. I didn't know who these people were, but they were of the same tribe as my people, as my twin brother, sister, uncles, aunts and cousins.

"Several days after we left that village I asked Abdul Kerim what language it was those people spoke among themselves. He said nothing for a long minute, and then he replied very slowly.

"'That is Aramaic, the language of the prophet Jesus. The people of that village who speak it are called Chaldeans,' he answered, and he gave me a long, penetrating look."

"And that is how I discovered I was Chaldean."

Jesus fell silent. A melancholic smile played with the corners of his mouth. His head bobbed up and down slowly, as if affirming his testimony.

I looked out the window at the tiled roof on the opposite side of the street. The light scent of geraniums wafted into the room. I hadn't been in a mosque for years, but felt, at that moment, as one might in a place of worship. Discovering who we are is, after all, an important religious act, isn't it? But what, I wondered, does one do with such knowledge?

The recorder clicked off, the room filled with silence.

74

Some Background

People are the products of their culture, and cultures are the products of history. For you to understand this story you need to know some of that history.

In 1913 a secret cabal in the Ottoman military, the so-called Committee of Truth and Progress, launched a coup against the Sultan, and the triumvirate of Enver, Jelal and Ismet Pashas formed the Young Turk government. Enver Pasha, as minister of defense, became the head of the Young Turk triumvirate. He made two huge mistakes. Firstly, during the First World War he allied our empire with Germany and Austria. Then, in 1914, during the war, Enver made his second grave mistake, an error that has affected us to the present. He ordered the eradication of the Armenian people.

This fate of the Armenians is a very sensitive subject in my country; acknowledging the fact that our forefathers committed genocide is considered seditious. I myself rejected the thought until recently. Let me explain.

The Ottoman Empire under the Sultan embraced numerous ethnic and racial groups. One of the largest of these, after the Turks, the Arabs and the Kurds, were the Armenians. Unlike the others, however, the Armenians were Christians. Enver Pasha feared, with some justification, that the Russians were inciting the Armenians by promising them an independent country on Ottoman

territory. Christian France and Britain were also suspected
of sending weapons to extremist Armenian groups. And so
Enver Pasha wired the fatal commands to his military
commanders . . .

After the war Enver Pasha escaped to Russia, where he
tried to incite the Turkic people of Central Asia against
the Communists. A Russian hit squad eventually assassi-
nated him. In the meantime, Mustafa Kemal's Nationalists
liberated Anatolia from the allied invaders and established
the Turkish Republic.

The Kemalist government, though not responsible for
the Armenian massacre, profited from the fact that
Anatolia's Armenian community had been largely eliminated. This was because Mustafa Kemal's own policy was
essentially racist as well: Turkey for the Turks. To this day,
in fact, the ruling establishment blindly refuses to
recognize that our country consists of a multiplicity of
coherent communities, each with its own identity. The
Nationalists responded to international calls for investigating the Armenian genocide by denying it ever
happened, a policy The General continues to follow.

∾∾∾

My relationship with Father, though not intimate, was
normally relaxed. There was even a sense of mutual
respect between us few of my friends could relate to.
Unlike their more domineering, arrogant or religiously
ideological fathers, my father had always given me a long
leash. We lived in quiet community; the tension which
existed for a couple of days after Father had left me so
brusquely, so uncharacteristically, was unusual, unwanted

by both of us. We soon fell into our regular routines, and it subsided, as I knew it would.

We were enjoying a cup of coffee some evenings later when I confronted him again.

"Dad, you pushed me into journalism," I said quietly, "and I thank you for it. You know I am good at my job; I am, after all, your son," I added disarmingly. "You know I can get to the bottom of who we are, that I can uncover whatever secrets you are determined to leave buried. Dad, tell me the truth and I won't need to dig elsewhere . . . "

Father pursed his lips and frowned. "That almost sounds like blackmail," he said, and I feared he'd clam up again. Instead he sighed. "I should have pushed you to become a lawyer instead," he said. "Don't wake the dead, my son," he added gently. "They will come to haunt you."

"If those dead are my forefathers, I'd like to know — irrespective of the consequences," I said quietly. "Aren't you the one who told me that truth leads to freedom?"

"Maybe I was wrong. Some truths enslave, not liberate," he said. His eyes had a faraway look about them.

"How can I, as a journalist, dig into other people's past while sticking my head in the sand with respect to my own?" I retorted.

He smiled weakly, approvingly, I thought, poured a whisky, and sunk deeper into his chair.

"As you like." He drained his glass, grimaced, and plunked it on the table. Then he began.

"You learned the main outlines of our family history from your grandmother, God bless her soul. Deranged as she was, her story was essentially true. Your grandfather was an evil man. The story goes back a generation before that, however, to his father. Your great-grandfather was a minor bureaucrat in Mardin, but early on he joined the secret Committee of Truth and Progress and played a key role at some stage of the revolt in the East. He was awarded the position of chief of postal works in Amîd for his services, which made him the *de facto* head of the local espionage system, to which the whole postal system was subordinated. In other words, he became a man of considerable influence.

"When mobilization orders reached Amîd, your great-grandfather secured a commission for your grandfather, who was in his teens at the time. He did not distinguish himself on the battlefield. He spent some time guarding the Hejaz railway, which the English spy Lawrence and his Arab irregulars were harassing. By the middle of the war he was back in Amîd, living at home. I don't know exactly what happened, because the subject of my father's behaviour during the war was taboo when I was a boy, but he had disgraced himself. Through your great-grandfather's connections he received a pardon for whatever it was he had done, and he joined the local militia as a second lieutenant. He was, however, no longer welcome in the homes of Amîd's better families.

"During the war orders reached your great-grandfather that they were to kill all the Armenians in the area. There had been no trouble with the poor wretches in the region, and he had no stomach for the order, yet he couldn't disobey it either. He obfuscated and procrastinated, but the orders had gone to the military and police chiefs as well. Anyway, he tried to play as low-key a part in the affair as he could get away with. He, in fact, became so disgusted with the Young Turks that he secretly switched his allegiance to Mustafa Kemal's Nationalists, another prescient move which stood him in good stead later.

"My father, on the other hand, saw an opportunity to redeem himself. He carried out the order with relish. Killing unarmed civilians was more to his taste than fighting Arab irregulars. He recruited Amîd's riffraff to built up his platoon until it swelled to a company. He and his men terrorized the countryside. He spurred his men to such excesses of behavior that he became known as The Butcher. They enriched themselves with loot and plunder."

It was the first time I had ever heard a Turk admit any culpability for the Armenian genocide. More than that, father even admitted that his own family — my family — played a role in the denied atrocity. I could barely believe my ears. I remember interrupting him and asking if he actually believed that we Turks had committed genocide.

"Yes, we did," he said flatly. A feeling of having been lied to invaded my being. Father smiled, not pleasantly. It was as if he was saying, "You wanted to know? Okay, here it is. Deal with it."

He picked up the narrative; his voice seemed to bore down on me.

"Your grandfather didn't limit his activities to Armenians. Under the guise of Holy War, he razed non-Armenian Christian villages as well. After one such raid he brought home a particularly beautiful Christian girl. He had raped her and she had pleased him, so he kept her as his slave, his concubine. Years later, in the late thirties, well after Mustafa Kemal had established the Republic, she became pregnant. At that point your great-grandfather made your grandfather marry the girl. That girl was your grandmother, Hanim, and I am the result of that union." Father poured himself another whisky before continuing.

"After the war there was a purge of Enver supporters. Your great-grandfather, however, kept his position as head of the Postal Services of Amîd, because he had secretly passed intelligence on to the Nationalists. Men like my father, who couldn't stop boasting of his exploits as the Butcher of the Armenians, became an embarrassment. He was ostracized. He also grew to hate my mother, the Christian plaything he had brought home and which had born him a son. The problem was that, although she had been forced to become a Muslim, she remained loyal to her Christian faith. She hated Muslims — understandably so. After all, her husband had killed her family, repeatedly raped her and forced her to accept the faith in whose name he had committed his atrocities. When I was a little boy she often whispered to me that Muslims were evil and Islam the doctrine of death, of Satan — just as she told you, no doubt, when I let you see her. I suppose her efforts at brainwashing me at that early stage had some effect. Islam has held no attraction for me. I must have communicated something to that effect, even back then, because the family refused to let me see my mother. They treated her like a pariah, keeping her locked in a back room for months on end. My father then married two other women, neither of whom wanted me.

"Anyway, I spent the first thirteen years of my life in my grandfather's house. I did reasonably well at school, and my grandfather got me into the prestigious Galatasaray Academy here in Istanbul. The rest you know. I studied law and set up my practice. I only went back to Amîd once, for my grandfather's funeral. When there, I was horrified to hear what my father had done to my mother some years earlier. He had her driven to Mardin, where there was still a sizable Christian community, and had her pushed out of the car in front of one of the churches.

"Mardin isn't a particularly large place, and when the police chief heard I was the grandson of Tarik Bey of Amîd, he put his men at my disposal. They located my mother in short order. She turned out to be a deranged beggar sitting beside the entrance of an old church. I brought her home to Istanbul."

Father's voice fell silent. He reached for a log and threw it into the fireplace. The fire crackled, a burst of flames disturbed the shadows, the spirited cadence of a Pagannini concerto laughing softly, mockingly, wafted from the stereo.

"Dad, does the name Hanbak mean anything to you?"

"I see that you've been doing your homework," he said with a wry face.

Extracts from Cassette #5, Side B:
Jesus Visits Amîd for the First Time

"I will never forget the first time we went to Amîd," Jesus began. 'We're running low on gold,' Abdul Kerim had said. 'We're going to Amîd to get more.'

"I became really excited! Amîd, Black Amîd! The Kurds call it Amîd, the Armenians; Dikranagerd, the Arabs; Diyar Bekir; and the Turks; Diyarbakir. It is the centre of our universe, the gateway to the world. It has guarded the northern Mesopotamian plateau as well as the passes into the Zagros Mountains since time immemorial. It draws its life from the great Tigris River, which all mankind knows because that mighty stream once flowed through Paradise. All the world has heard of Amîd's great, black basalt walls, second only to the Great Wall of China, and everyone knows of the smoking domes of its public baths, and of the multitude of minarets and steeples scraping the sky, simultaneously carrying their respective messages upward, heavenward!"

I smiled inwardly. The old man was reliving days almost a century ago. He was, once again, a village boy struck with the wonders of the capital of Kurdistan. His voice, though feeble, rose with excitement.

"We approached the city from the northwest, from the White Mountains. It took several days to descend the mountains and cross the plain. It was summer; the sun had

82

turned into a ball of fire, burning and scorching all below it. We followed the curves of the upper reaches of the Tigris. The river, cascading and surging turbulently in the spring, was reduced to a sluggish stream. It was terribly hot; you didn't have to go elsewhere to find out what hell was like. Even the bougainvilleas were brown and wilted. Then, one day, Amîd's walls became visible, shimmering in the distance through the heat-haze.

"There were a few flat-roofed, hard-packed, dirt houses dotted along the curves of the road leading up to the walls, and I remember thinking that living there must be the next thing to living in heaven itself. There were fresh vegetables growing all around — lettuces, tomatoes, beans, cabbages and melons larger than any I had ever seen — with the city just above!"

Jesus' eyes were closed and he was shaking his head as he relived the wonders of that day. Then he broke into a cackling laugh. He opened his eyes and his head bobbed up and down with mirth.

"Suddenly a huge black monster catapulted out of the city gate and hurled down the hill. It rushed straight at us. Then it roared with a terrible, high-pitched, unnatural noise. Grey and black smoke spewed from its rear end. Abdul Kerim turned and shouted, 'Get out of its way! Hold on to your animal!' But I was too scared. I stood in its path, frozen with terror, clutching my donkey's mane. An acrid stench filled the air. Then, to my utter astonishment, I saw a man sitting inside the metal monster! The beast let out another horrible blast and veered around my donkey and me.

"All at once my petrified donkey jolted to life. It leapt from the road, and tore across the tomato fields as though the devil himself was chasing it. I hung on for dear life. When, eventually, the animal finally halted, all was quiet again — quiet, except for the poor beast's and my heavy panting, and the peals of laughter rolling across the field. Abdul Kerim was doubled over and slapping his thighs, as though he had just witnessed the funniest spectacle ever!"

Jesus' eyes were sparkling as he laughed. On the tape you can hear his pinched chest heaving from the effort.

"I had heard of the existence of these carts which moved like the wind without horse or ox or mule to pull them along," Jesus continued, "but I had dismissed the notion as impossible. My head spun and I wondered what other miracles Amîd had in store for me.

"Well, we entered through the New Gate. It was extremely busy inside the walls. I was afraid I'd lose Abdul Kerim, and stuck to him like a shadow. The crowd flowed like water around us.

"Myriads of haggling women, sharp-eyed street urchins, and suspicious-looking men crowded the alleyways. Shawls, carpets and laundry were strung from ropes overhead and alternately light and dark swept over us as we moved from cool stretches of shade into patches of blazing sunlight.

"Abdul Kerim knew Amîd well. We threaded our way among cursing merchants shooing bundled pack mules, waddling women balancing oversized parcels on their heads, and perspiring servants puffing under the weight of drab litters concealing overweight dignitaries or high-class women. Street musicians prodded their dancing bears and impish monkeys, beat their drums, strummed their lutes, or blew into their horns. Hawkers, shrill and sonorous, advertised their wares. The din was overwhelming.

"We walked through the narrow, shop-lined streets, cutting this way and that through the throng, darting from swinging elbows, dodging descending hooves, coming up for air in short-lived pockets of space. Abdul Kerim made his way down one street and up another until my mind was numb. We eventually entered the courtyard of a small inn where we tied up our beasts for the night. Abdul Kerim shared his bread with me, and then I fell exhausted onto the pallet in the room we shared with a dozen others.

"The following morning Abdul Kerim told me to take care of myself, because he had business to tend to. I worked my way back to the teeming market, where I saw sights I'd never seen before. One of the first things that struck me were the mounds of food! I had never before seen — or even imagined — the incredible variety of fruits and vegetables that filled the market tables to overflowing. There were stacks of bright oranges, shiny red apples, silver squashes and yellow gourds. There were piles of green spinach and heaps of red, orange and green peppers. There were stalls where they only sold dried foods, such as different kinds of rice, corn and nuts. Other stalls only sold spices: large, jute bags full of ginger, cinnamon, cloves, cardamom, jasmine, cumin and myrtle imparted a tangy, intoxicating quality to the air. I walked past pyramids of pungent cheeses, briny pools of olives, mounds of shelled almonds and baskets of lentils. Moneychangers, their cash stored in vaults behind them, exchanged dinars, liras and rials. Shops and stalls were so full of merchandise that their shining brass and copper pots, cooking bowls and water jars spilled out onto the street. Other stores were stacked high with bolts of brightly coloured cloth and finely embroidered shawls. Yet others sold soaps and attars, lanterns, umbrellas, shoes, carpets, bales of tobacco, wood . . . I hardly knew where to look, everything was so new, so wonderful. Here, all the people of the Zagros Mountains mixed and mingled. I'd heard it said that if you sat long enough in the Bazaar of Amîd, you'd eventually see everyone who lived in Kurdistan. I found that easy to believe.

"I observed the faces of the people around me. There were the Kurdish women wearing their numerous layers of red, yellow and green, chattering happily as they haggled with some harassed Jew while their haughty menfolk, wearing towering turbans and tightly knotted cummerbunds, looked on. There were Arabs wearing white robes and red *kafiyes* with black *egals*. There were swarthy farmers, their baggy trousers lolloping as they strode along. There were short, squat Turks, their wives covered in the drab black of the chador. I loved it all as I stood in the middle of the buzzing, swirling, throbbing, pulsating market.

"Then I smelled a wonderful smell, a smell more delicious than anything I'd ever smelled before. I followed my nose through the throng to a stall where a man was sitting on a low stool with a large black kettle bubbling on a low, charcoal burner. Paying no attention to the swarms of flies around him, he concentrated on the boiling syrup he was stirring slowly. I watched with fascination as he languidly lifted a copper ladle full of the goo from the pot and poured some onto a sheet of flattened tin, twirling it into butterfly-like shapes. He let the shapes cool and then placed them onto the mound of amber butterflies beside him.

"'How much, my uncle?' I asked.

"'One *qurush*.'

"I gave him the copper, grasped my golden butterfly and carried it gingerly to a quiet spot in the shade of the city wall. There I found an oleander bush, sat underneath and slowly nibbled my butterfly, savouring every bite. I decided then that somehow, at some time, I would return to Amîd to stay. For everyone eventually passes through Amîd . . .

"I don't remember exactly how long Abdul Kerim and I remained there, but it must have been about a week or ten days — long enough, in any case, for me to get to know the city. While Abdul Kerim went about his business, I climbed the black basalt walls and joined the storks that made their nests there. From there the Tigris looked like a brown rope looped along the valley floor. I could also see the domes of the public baths and the minarets of the sprawling city, and could soon identify the Pasha Bath, the Camel Bath, and the Chardakli Bath as well as the Yîkîk minaret and the four-footed minaret.

"I didn't just fall in love with Amîd because it embraced every miracle and good thing invented by mankind. No, there was more to it than that. Unlike the other towns and villages, which consisted of one or, at best, two communities — Alawite and Yezidi or Turkish and Armenian or Syriac and Kurdish or whatever — Amîd's walls embraced them all, though each group lived in its own quarter. Among that pulsating kaleidoscope of people I believed that there must be someone who knew the whereabouts of my kin. Amîd fanned the hope lit when we visited the Chaldean village.

"I discovered that the Armenians lived in the Hanchepek district of the Infidel Quarter. The Armenians all worked as craftsmen. All the metalworkers of Amîd, for instance, were Armenians. Ironmongery had been passed on from father to son for generations among them, as though by command of the Sultan. They beat their red-hot iron into shovels, plows, axes, doorknobs, hinges, nails, animal traps, and a thousand other artifacts. Virtually all the shoemakers and stone-carvers were also Armenians. Whatever the craft, you'd find a majority of Armenians among them. Among them a person's trade often served as part of his name: Bedo the kettle maker; Nigogus the stove-maker; Vanes the tinsmith; Istepan the blacksmith; Carpenter Nisho; Tailor Antramik; Hello the bag-maker; Sarkis the dentist; Hajo the tinker. If two people with the same name worked at the same trade, one would be identified by some physical characteristic, such as Sarkis, the cross-eyed carpenter.

"The Jews, the Armenian's neighbours, lived around the New Gate or, to be more precise, between Infidel Quarter, Infidel Square and the New Gate. You wouldn't find a single Armenian, Turk or Kurd living in their district. Unlike the Armenians, the Jews were all merchants. The word 'Jew', in fact, was synonymous with 'merchant'. Even the poorest among them, those too poor to open a store, would become merchants. They'd sling a burlap sack over their shoulders and walk the streets shouting, 'Empty bottles! Empty bottles! I'll take your empty bottles!' Or, 'Flour for sale! Finely ground flour!' Or, 'Used clothes! Used clothes bought and sold!' Or, 'Old shoes for sale! Old shoes bought and sold!'

"The wealthier Jews owned stores on Melki Ahmet Boulevard, from where they sold glassware, hardware, china, rock salt, wool, olive oil, crocheting needles, hairpins, scissors, balls of string, ground coconut, orchid roots, canvas, and a thousand other objects. Every evening you could hear a loud, metallic clanging and banging up and down Melki Ahmet Boulevard as the Jews pulled down their roll-down shutters and clicked countless deadbolts and padlocks into place before scurrying home with the day's profit.

"To get from Melki Ahmet Boulevard to their own quarter they had to walk past the fisherman's stalls, turn left at the four-footed minaret and pass through Hanchepek, the Armenian district of Infidel Quarter. That was the shortest route. In the summer they preferred a longer route through the back streets in order to avoid the 'sons of the Christian bitches' lurking in doorways and alleys looking forward to bombarding the Jews with the profusion of melon peels which littered the streets at that time of the year.

"The Syriacs lived in their own quarter in the west of the city between the Hamediye and Mardin gates. The centre of their world was the historic Mother Mary Syriac church. They were extremely proud of the fact that they were among the world's first Christians. They were also very proud of the religious knowledge and zeal of their priests. The fastest way to ingratiate one's self with their priests was to ask them about their past. 'We are an old Semitic race,' they'd intone. 'Our church was founded in Antioch by St. Peter himself. That's why we are known as the Old Syriac church.'

"Just as everyone has his own way of eating yogurt, and just like every chicken cackles in its own peculiar way, the Syriacs had their own ways of doing things. When passing through their quarter most people wouldn't be able to understand a word of the language their womenfolk shouted from the doorways and windows across the narrow alleyways.

"If the Armenians had no competition in the field of ironmongery, the same could be said of the Syriacs with respect to goldsmithing. They carefully kept their trade secrets to themselves, taking only boys from their own community as apprentices. Those who weren't involved in jewellry-making, raised silk worms or entered the textile business. Their shops were near the wheat market; the brightly coloured fabrics were much sought after by Kurdish women. There were also Syriac communities outside of Amîd, in the towns of Midyat and Mardin. Their largest monastery was, in fact, in Mardin. It is called Deir ul Zaferan."

Jesus fell silent. He looked down, clasped his hands, and then unclasped them again. I wondered what was coming. When he started speaking he didn't look at me.

"One afternoon, after we'd been in the city for several days, I entered an alley near the Sheikh Matar mosque. Two men, one with loose-hanging jowls, were slaughtering a goat. I watched as one of them cut the beast's throat while the other held its head back to allow the still-pumping heart to drain out the blood. The man with the jowls then inserted a little metal tube into a slit he'd cut into one of the hind legs and began blowing for all he was worth. As he blew the animal slowly started to inflate, and its skin began peeling off the carcass.

"The man's face strained with effort, his cheeks swelling to the size of Amîd's melons and his eyes protruded 'til I thought they'd pop from their sockets. It was a funny sight, and I burst out laughing."

A ripple fluttered across Jesus' body and a smile flashed over his face.

"The man doing the blowing tried to scowl, which made him even funnier. His friend picked up a rock. *'Gi tovarno agarmeghug!'*, he shouted. "I'll break every bone in your body!" I started sprinting away when, all at once, something clicked. I stopped running, turned around, and slowly walked back towards them. I wasn't laughing anymore.

"The second man still had the rock in his hand. *'Mobil hathe le mug!'* 'Take that to your mother!' I dodged the stone with ease but kept looking at them from a distance. The man looked down at his pal and said loud enough for me to hear, *'Hano dayvonoyo'*. That means 'the kid is crazy' in the language the children of the village on the Habur River were chattering among themselves . . .

"That is how I discovered the Chaldean quarter where, eventually, I really came to understand who my people were . . . "

Jesus' head waggled up down for a while. Then he let out a long, audible sigh, looked up at me, smiled wanly, and continued.

"We Chaldeans, like the Syriacs and Armenians, are also an ancient Christian people. I remember entering their solemn church for the first time. This was much later, after I'd run away from Abdul Kerim. The Chaldean church stood near the Armenian Surp Girgaros church. When you entered its portal you first stepped into a large courtyard, which you had to cross to reach a second, smaller door. It opened into the vestibule. Like the people who went in before me, I dipped my hand into a marble basin filled with holy water and daubed some on my face. Then I entered the sanctuary. The first thing that struck me were the large oil paintings of Jesus, Mary, the disciples, and of sundry saints hanging everywhere, which years of candle smoke, moisture and mildew had blackened. One particular painting really impressed me. It was a huge picture of the Last Supper. Jesus, his face lit by the halo over his head, was breaking bread, and handing it to his disciples. I knelt before the altar and prayed the Aramaic Lord's Prayer. Although I later visited that church regularly, I could never figure out which disciple was Judas the Betrayer. There were also crosses, Bibles, and candleholders.

"Although the Chaldean community was small, it controlled the spice and perfume market. If you needed ginger, cloves, citric acid, black pepper, coriander, allspice or any kind of sweet smelling perfumes or attars you could be sure get it from Perfumer Joseph on Gazi Boulevard. And if he didn't have it, Aziz Anbar's store near the Mardin Gate would be certain to stock it.

"The Turks, for their part, either worked for the government or in the medical profession. The governor, judges, lawyers, the police, teachers, soldiers, officially licensed doctors, midwives, nurses, dentists and pharmacists were all Turks.

"The Kurds lived in the surrounding villages. Most of them were farmers, though a few wealthy Kurdish landowners lived in large villas within the city walls. You could see village Kurds leading their donkeys and mules, trying to sell the firewood they'd cut in the forests. You could also hear them in the summer as they wandered the streets carrying huge clay water pots shouting, 'Cold water! Cold water for sale!'"

At this point a passing vehicle with muffler problems makes Jesus' words unintelligible. When the recording picks him up again, he had moved on to the subject of religion, something he talked about with dry, wry wit.

"Although the people of Amîd all served the same God, they approached the problem of acccss to him differently. Some worshipped in mosques, some in churches, some in synagogues. The *muezzin* and the church bell competed every couple of hours to see who would reach the Golden Throne first. That competitive spirit was also evident architecturally: Muslims and Christians vied to build the highest edifice in town, so, consequently, the city boasted numerous minarets and stceples.

"In the rivalry for God's ear the Muslims met on Fridays in thc Great Mosque or in one of the local mosqucs or, if they were Alawites, in one of their meeting houses. The Alawites must have been surer of their standing with God than either Sunni or Shia Muslims or the Christians, because their mcctinghouses didn't have minarets or stceples. The Christians, on the other hand, met in one of Amîd's myriad of churches. There were a mind-boggling number of different kinds of Christians in Amîd. There were the Catholics, who insisted that the way to God ran through Rome. Then there were the Protestants, who held that there we no detours in the road to the Almighty. The Orthodox also held that theirs was the only way, while the Gregorians proclaimed that they were the first to accept Christianity en mass. And, of course, there were the Syriac, Chaldean, and Nestorian churches as well. There were also those who sought to find the right way through yet other ways. The Jews, for instance, claimed that they had clung to the notion of the one, true, God longer than all the others. They were also practitioners of the oldest religious instruction of all: an eye for an eye and a tooth for a tooth. A small group of Yezidis worshipped their Peacock Angel, while the Zoroastrians worshipped fire, and the few Druze who passed through worshipped a deranged caliph of the eleventh century. Some sensitive souls eventually found their way to Sufism. They became followers of Ibn Arabi, or Mevlana irRumi, or Umr al Fadil. They strove for union with God.

"Anyone who didn't belong to your own particular community or religious affiliation was considered an infidel. It was impossible to change communities or religious affiliation. Whatever community you were born into was yours for life. That was how God, in His infinite wisdom, decreed it. Anyone who tried to switch allegiance went against the very order of the universe."

Jesus fell silent. His last couple of sentences hung heavily in the air.

Who Am I?

My father, as I said, is a well-known lawyer. We live in an affluent suburb. I received the best education our country has to offer and spent my holidays in our villa on the Mediterranean. My friends and colleagues were from the same milieu. After work, we chummed at one of the fashionable cafés on Independence Avenue, and on weekends we played basketball or squash.

I spent much professional energy keeping a close tab on economic trends. I also had a habit of pursuing stories pertaining to the graft and corruption of men close to The General, a practice that was giving me something of a profile in media circles. Whenever I had the urge I dated one of *The Morning*'s better-looking secretaries, or took her down to our villa for the weekend. Life was comfortable, yet meaningful. With the quiet support of Father I felt I was beginning to contribute to the hard-pressed democratic movement in our country.

I was a member of the monied, upper-class minority. I was, of course, aware of the lot of my fellow citizens — it was impossible not to be familiar with the street urchins and beggars sitting on the side of the road exaggerating their deformities by squatting in some impossible position, their doleful eyes seeking contact. They were an irritation, an embarrassment to the tourists who brought much needed foreign currency into the country. One of The

General's more positive acts were his periodic attempts to clear the streets of beggars.

Poverty, to me, was an abstraction. I knew the reports and the statistics, and had even written some eloquent articles on the subject, though with no more feeling, no more empathy, than if I'd been dealing with the economy or sports. The poorest people I knew personally were our cook, cleaning lady and doorman. They were always well dressed and polite. The only thing I knew about them was that each had a spouse and an indefinite number of children. In my country, people from our class don't mix with the lower classes — not because we consider ourselves inherently superior, but simply because we don't have much in common with them.

If the topic of poverty remained largely academic, the subject of minorities cut closer to the bone. After all, my own grandmother, God bless her soul, was some kind of ethnic minority. The minorities issue, as you know by now, is an extremely sensitive subject here. Kurdish terrorist organizations tormented us for years and, like most of my colleagues, I agreed with The General — it was about the only subject we agreed with him on — that extreme measures were needed to deal with that troublesome issue. After all, the integrity of the state was at stake.

The former Ottoman Empire embraced Turks and Syrians, Egyptians and Iraqis, Berbers, Kurds, Armenians, Greeks, Bulgarians, Romanians, Circassians, Laz, Turcomen and countless others. However, the desire of different minority groups to establish their own nation-states on Ottoman soil, and the aid they received to this end from the great European powers, led to the disintegration of the empire. The Greeks, the Bulgarians, and the Romanians all broke away during the nineteenth century. During the First World War the Arabs, incited by the British, also broke away. Of the former empire, once the largest in the world, nothing was left but the rump state of Anatolia, ancient Asia Minor.

My interviews with Jesus opened my eyes to many things. First of all, poverty ceased to be an abstraction: Jesus and Shimone gave it a human face, and the district they lived in put it on the map. In time I would take advantage of my free passage into the area to wander the tangle of streets, sip tea in coffeehouses, buy odds and ends at corner stores, and listen to the gossip. I was determined to get to know the area, because I came to realize that a certain type of knowledge can only come from the grass roots, a knowledge which would add colour, flavour, and intimacy to my writing and research.

The now forgotten Melki had done me a great service by introducing me to Jesus, for Jesus not only put a human face to poverty and suffering, he also drew a fascinating picture of the history of our country. His stories were so transparent, so obviously true, that they moved me deeply. He was a born storyteller. He could paint scenes of things he'd witnessed nearly a century ago and tell them as if he were reliving them at that moment. He gave me a history of our country from a "bottom up" perspective which no academic, no historian could have achieved. I didn't mind his many digressions and descriptions. This was living history. I determined that someday I would edit that growing collection of tapes and write a book about that tragic, heroic, lost era. This is that book.

∾∾∾

"Dad, remember, I told you about this old codger I am inter-viewing on The Hill? He's called Jesus; Jesus the Infidel. I'm recording his life story. It's a fascinating, living history of the twentieth century as seen through the perspective of a unique man."

"What's so unique about him?"

"He is the last Chaldean male alive in our country. When he dies, 4000 years of history dies with him."

"And he interests you because your grandmother was Chaldean."

"You never told me that!" I exclaimed. "I only knew she was Christian."

"You found out from your little man in the archives," Father said evenly.

"How do you know that?" I was surprised, shocked. "Are you having my phone tapped?" I demanded angrily.

He laughed. "No, not yet," he said, "though I may have to if you pursue this Jesus thing much further. You are likely to bring down the house on both of us. As for your first question, did you think Mr. Mehmet Shimshek would pass classified information to a green reporter of *The Morning*, if you had been anyone else's son? He informs me of everything he passes on to you. And if he wonders whether the information is suitable, he asks me first. Mr. Mehmet Shimshek and I go back a long, long way," he added dryly.

I felt humiliated. Why hadn't I realized the obvious ages ago, I asked myself. Was it because I had inflated my own importance? I should have questioned why Mr. Shimshek included me among his select clique of safe journalists. All of a sudden it dawned on me that Father must have asked him to. Why? To settle his own scores, scores I knew nothing about? The cunning old fox had been manipulating me for his own unfathomable purposes.

I was quiet for a while. Father resumed typing into the computer. Mozart's *Violin Concerto in G Minor* hung in the air. A log broke in two, sending a shower of sparks up the chimney. I got off the couch and walked to the picture window. It was cold and dark outside.

"Dad, do you know anything about minority groups?" A steady drizzle beat against the panes.

"Which ones?" My father looked at me over the top of his laptop.

"Those in the South-East."

"I know a bit." The waters of the Bosphorus were choppy, their whitecaps reflecting the lights of a passing freighter.

"Tell me what you know about the Christian minority groups down there," I asked quietly.

Father typed a few more words, then shut down the computer. He got up, stretched, threw a fresh log onto the fire, walked to the bar and poured himself a whisky.

"Do you want a drink?" he asked.

"No thanks."

He picked up the tumbler and headed for his leather armchair. "You'd better get your little tape-recorder, because it's a complicated story," he said.

I went to my room and fetched the machine. When I got back Father slouched in his chair; his head was tilted back, his eyes closed, his hands grasped the whisky glass and his feet were planted on the coffee table.

"I'm ready," I said.

More Background

Rather than transcribe my father's explanations, I prefer my own words. Not that what he said was not accurate. It was. I was able confirm what he said later. In fact, the research I did, based on what he told me, enables me to give this more detailed account.

The ancient Chaldeans converted to Islam in the seventh and eighth centuries AD, assimilated into the Arab/Muslim culture, and disappeared from history. When the Byzantine Empire fell to the Ottoman Turks in the fifteenth century, Muslims came to rule over the Armenian, Nestorian, and Orthodox churches.

The Armenian and Orthodox churches were national institutions of the Armenians and Greeks, while someone called Nestorius had founded the Nestorian church in the fifth century. He apparently disagreed with the teaching that the Virgin Mary was the mother of God as well as the mother of Christ, so he was excommunicated and started his own church. Anyway, for centuries these three groups lived as recognized *millets*, Christian minority groups, within the larger, Ottoman society.

In the 1550s a group of Nestorians wanted to rejoin the Roman Catholic church. The Vatican, for some mysterious reason, started calling these people Chaldeans. In other words, Melki's notion that Jesus the Infidel was the last male of a culture that goes back 4000 years is hogwash.

There is no link, though people think there is because the Aramaic spoken by this later Chaldean community evolved differently from that of other Aramaic speaking tribes, because nineteenth century Anglican missionaries confused the matter, and because it suited the nationalist aspirations of some during the last days of the Ottoman Empire.

I mentioned Anglicans. They're a branch of Protestantism. From the early 1800s onward all kinds of Protestant missionaries headed for the Ottoman Empire. They came with a desire to work among the Muslims, but found that hard going. When they discovered that ancient churches survived in the region, they revised their strategy. They opted to work with these churches in the hope that, in time, these would shoulder the burden of taking Christianity to their Muslim neighbours. Strengthening the existing churches became a substitute for their failure to evangelize Muslims — though they convinced themselves that they were still pursuing the same end, but by a different means.

Anyways, the Protestants built a large network of schools and hospitals. They also established printing presses, which churned out parts of the Bible along with newspapers and educational books. The missionaries believed that even as Islam had steam-rolled over a nominal Christendom in the seventh century, so reviving the orthodox churches would roll it back. But instead of reviving the ancient churches they split them, so they formed "evangelical" Protestant churches.

Wave after wave of missionaries, mostly American, came and worked in the heart of Islam, but not among Muslims. They continued evangelizing impressive numbers of Orthodox Christians, who were absorbed into the newly-formed, western-led evangelical denominations. They failed to see that their activities would lead to the destruction of Christendom in our country.

The sudden interest of all those westerners in unimportant, servile tribes — who had managed to prolong their existence only because of their insignificance and the remoteness of their habitat — stirred the suspicions of many. The Kurds, in particular, viewed the empowerment of subservient Christians as a possible first step leading to their own overthrow. In other words, the missionaries, in their innocent ignorance, set the stage for reprisals.

Another factor, one the missionaries themselves were only dimly aware of was that they arrived in Anatolia just when a power struggle was taking place between the Sultan in Constantinople and local landlords, the aghas. Before the 1840s these aghas had acted as rulers over virtually independent fiefdoms. They'd collected their own taxes and commanded their own militias. They owned their Christian peasants, who were bought and sold with the land they worked. After the 1840s, however, the Sultan was able to increase his power. He banished a number of these aghas to Western Turkey, Damascus, and elsewhere, and replaced them with Turkish governors, with whom he could be in direct contact through the newly laid telegraph lines.

All the while the missionaries were lobbying on behalf of their co-religionists by writing endless streams of letters to their embassies and to sympathetic politicians in Europe and America. Although they maintained that they did not represent any earthly powers, neither their own Christian disciples nor the Muslims saw it that way. In fact, the local Kurds regarded the missionary compounds as forts; the imported windows, for example, the first ever seen in the region, were assumed to be portholes for snipers. Centralized authority, western missionary activity, and the rising expectations of the Christian serfs created increasingly greater anxiety among the Muslim tribes.

Within a decade after the arrival of the missionaries the first massacres took place. The Kurds slaughtered thousands in the villages the missionaries had targeted. The central government in Constantinople turned a blind eye, because it also suspected the missionaries of fomenting a Christian separatist movement. Many were killed, untold others sold into slavery. These massacres, which lasted from 1843 to 1846, were the first of numerous conflicts between Christians and Muslims in modern times.

It's hard to determine how much blame the missionaries bore. The local Kurds had been making life miserable for Christians long before the missionaries arrived. Destroying their crops, raiding their villages, and taking their women was a national pastime. However, the Kurds suspected, and the missionaries seemed to confirm by their actions if not their words, that Christians from the west and the Christians of Kurdistan were forming a political alliance.

Whatever the truth of these matters is, people don't respond to facts; they react to impressions.

"We arrived back in Bezal in the late autumn, and spent the winter there. Grandfather had passed away in our absence. He lay buried beside grandmother on the slope behind the house. That was the last winter I would spend with Abdul Kerim, Mother Ayshe and Reward.

"I had grown to love Abdul Kerim and Mother Ayshe. They had saved my life, and treated me as if I was their real son. Reward thought I was his older brother. The prospect of running away from them in the spring weighed very heavily on me the whole length of that long, cold winter. Yet I had no choice. They were not my people.

"It is true that I lived as a Muslim. Certainly everyone in the mountain villages thought of me as such. I prayed with Abdul, went to the mosque on Fridays and kept Ramadan. Whenever we were back in Bezal the villagers didn't bother me, though they never tried to be my friends — not even the young guys my own age. They couldn't forget that our house had collapsed and they sensed that, in my heart, I wasn't a true believer. They didn't bother me because nothing bad had happened to the village since I started roaming with Abdul Kerim. The Evil Eye had been averted and, if I didn't hang around too long, would probably leave them alone. But I couldn't overstay my welcome. So long as they knew I was only there temporarily everything was okay.

"The villagers were right. Ever since I discovered who I was I hoped that I would be re-united with my own people. These things being so, I really was a potential channel for bad spiritual forces to the people of Bezal.

"You see, in Kurdistan people don't mix. Two communities might live in one village and share the same well, yet invisible fences separate them. Each community is a nation with its own history, religion, pride, language and shared suffering. Were someone to switch from the one to the other he would change the spiritual dynamic as well as betray his people and break his father's heart. One did not consider switching communities any more than one would consider changing one's sex. It was something that went against the laws of nature, against the rules with which God and Jesus and the prophets bound the earth. It was a crime against humanity, no, more than a crime; it was a sin against God on high! The crash of Abdul Kerim's house was incontrovertible proof to the villagers that God disapproved of his adopting me into their midst.

"Though I knew that Abdul Kerim himself did not feel about me the way the other villagers did, and though Mother Ayshe believed that God rewarded their mercy to me by granting her Reward, I felt I had to leave. They didn't drive me out, nor was it something I discussed with them. I simply knew I had to go. I had to find my own people, or I feared I would, in time, bring another evil on Abdul Kerim's household and possibly on the whole village.

"I had to leave them for their own good but also for my eternal well-being. For how could I, for my part, keep on living in unpardonable sin? Just because people look alike doesn't mean you judge them by the same standards! Just because small turnips look like large radishes doesn't mean they are the same things. You don't harvest pears and apples from the same tree, or honeydew and watermelons off the same field. Also, not trying to reunite with my own people would break my dead parents' hearts and cause me to burn in hell.

"The thought of leaving the warmth and safety of Abdul Kerim and Mother Ayshe distressed me very much. I knew my departure would grieve them deeply too, but what could I do? They wanted to think of me as their son, but I was someone else's son . . . "

Jesus' voice died down and that melancholic smile tugged at his mouth. I'd listened with fascination to the contorted cosmology of superstitious villagers. At the same time I couldn't help but wonder if there were powers beyond the theology of orthodox Islam. Was there, at some level, truth to such spiritual realities and dark unseen forces as the jinn and the Evil Eye?

I hadn't thought much about the Evil Eye before, though in our country the blue beads used to help ward off its influence are hung in every house and office, tacked to every vehicle, pinned to every baby, and worn by virtually all women on their necklaces or bracelets. I had a big plastic one hanging in my office, and knew that I would feel vulnerable if it were removed. If I, a modern, secular, Turkish intellectual, could feel that kind of vulnerability, surely those credulous villagers of Bezal would too! What Jesus had just explained made perfect sense . . .

"I have many good memories — snippets, really, of unimportant yet precious memories — of that last winter with Abdul Kerim and Mother Ayshe and Reward," Jesus continued. He looked away from me and out of the window, beyond the geraniums and into the past. He remained quiet and I feared that he wouldn't pick up the thread of his story. I needed him to finish.

"Tell me some of those snippets of good memories," I coaxed. He was silent for a little longer, then turned to face me again.

"Imagine a blizzard raging outside," he began. "Abdul Kerim, Mother Ayshe, Reward, maybe some of the neighbours — Uncle Shelo and Aunt Hatije — and I are all sitting cross-legged on the floor around the large copper tray. There was no such thing as setting the table in those days. Food was served on the copper tray, and eaten straight from the big pan. If God had blessed us that day with barley porridge, there would be barley porridge in the pan, and if, in His mercy, he gave lentil soup, there'd be lentil soup in it.

"Now imagine the pan full of rice mixed with mutton braised in its own fat. Outside a blizzard is attacking the chimney. You can see nothing but white out of the window, which the wind is attacking furiously, futilely. The kerosene lamp is full, its wick trimmed, the wood-stove is burning red as a pomegranate, the crackling flames are background music. You rip a piece off the bread and use it to scoop a helping of meat and rice which you stuff into your mouth. Mother Ayshe hands you a raw onion and you bite a piece off it as well. Is there anything better than that?" Jesus' eyes sparkled as he described the simple domestic scene.

"You eat your fill, then Mother Ayshe collects the remnants of bread and wipes the pot and tray clean. Reward stuffs another log into the stove. Abdul Kerim nods half asleep in a corner, Aunt Hatije is darning a stocking, and you are picking a sliver of meat from your teeth using a stalk snapped off the whiskbroom. Afterwards, while the snow rises waist-high, you gather around the copper tray to crack walnuts and drink coffee. You tell me, what can be more wonderful?"

"Or listen to this: one day that winter Abdul Kerim, Uncle Shelo, their son Baran, Reward and I went to cut firewood. We tied our axes and ropes to Abdul's horse and headed for the forests above Bezal.

"It was a crisp, clear day, one of those days when nothing could go wrong. We cut a huge pile of firewood, enough to last both households for weeks. We figured it would take us at least three days to haul it all down to the village.

"It was after dark when we finally set off for home. There was a full moon, and there were no clouds in the night sky; a needle would have shone in that darkness. We could make out the foxholes on either side of the trail and could see the dark silhouette of Mount Judy. We sang as we marched home. We were tired with the satisfying weariness that comes from honest labour.

"We were walking single file through the narrow Mehmediye Pass. Uncle Shelo was in front, holding the horse's reins, the rest of us trailed after him. Then, unexpectedly, Uncle Shelo stopped dead in his tracks. He pulled the horse to a halt and stood there, still as a statue, one hand up in the air as a warning. We tiptoed to where he was standing and what did we see? There, in the middle of the trail, lay two huge bears. None of us had ever seen bears that big. The creatures that normally roamed our area seemed like pups compared to these monsters. They lay motionless, their huge bodies etched against the snow-bank behind them. Their noses were touching. They were simply gargantuan. Where had they come from? Worst of all, they blocked the road. How in the world could we get around them? You'd have to climb over them to get through the pass.

"'Look,' Uncle Shelo whispered. 'They're sleeping.'

"'If they wake up we're done for.'

"'What should we do?' Reward whimpered.

"'Look at their size!' Abdul Kerim whispered awestruck. 'I've never seen anything like it. Look at their backs. They're the length of table-tops.'

"'Oh no,' Baran moaned. "Look, the one on the left is getting up. We must have woken it . . . No, he's sitting down again. Look . . . What can we do?'

"'Let's go back and spend the night in the forest,' I suggested. 'They'll be gone by morning.'

"But that suggestion fell flat. The men had their honour to maintain. If they didn't return, they'd become the laugh-ingstock of the village.

"'Let's stone them,' Uncle Shelo whispered. 'Let's rush at them shouting and screaming and throw stones. Maybe that'll scare them and make them run away. If they attack us, defend yourself with your ax.' Everyone agreed that this was the thing to do.

"We each grabbed a large rock with one hand and grasped our axes in the other, then rushed the bears, shouting at the top of our lungs. I was so scared I pissed my pants. The bears didn't budge. When we got within striking range we threw our rocks, but the bears still didn't move. Uncle Shelo raised his hand again, and crept up to the nearest one. All of a sudden he straightened out and split the frozen air with laughter.

"'They're not bears, boys,' he shouted between guffaws. We crowded toward him, to discover that the stupendous bears were nothing more than two bushes which had been cut at the stem and dropped in the middle of the pass. How had they gotten there? We never found out. They'd probably fallen off some woodcutter's cart."

SHIMONE

I said earlier that The Hill's narrow alleys and streets intimidated me. Taxis refused to enter the slum beyond the red-light area, so I always had to climb the last stretch to Jesus' house alone.

There was a disturbing loneliness about those alleys that contrasted starkly to the pleasantly reassuring hustle of the boutiques, art galleries and cafés near my own house. Here pedestrians scuffled hurriedly up or down the hill to vanish quickly into some crumbling building or another. I would walk fast, clutching the bag containing my cassette recorder and tapes close to my chest, until I reached the house where Jesus stayed.

After the interview I'd quickly thread my way back down the dark, deserted streets to the lower reaches of the district. There flashing red lights bursting from the display windows, brightly lit nightclubs and cabarets, and neon signs dispelled the darkness. Once there, I competed for a cab with men who had finished their business behind the sagging doorways. Not until it had left the dockside area and was speeding down the ring road would I begin to relax.

That changed as my sense of unease decreased. I started arriving earlier to let Hampar the Armenian cut my hair and trim my beard, or to let Misto the Gypsy polish my shoes. Andreas Stephanopolis might sell me a bottle of

Coke, or make me a cheese sandwich, and Shukru the
Alawite would insist on buying me a glass of tea from
Mahmut the Arab who ran the coffeehouse. I learned that
the Armenian Hampar had four ugly, unmarried daughters;
that Misto's wife and sons collected orange peels from the
big hotels which they sold to a marmalade factory; that Ali
was a widower whose son studied sociology at the
university; and, that Mahmut's wife had left him because
she'd gotten tired of being beaten nightly. Aziz the porter
always asked how I was, then commented politely on the
weather as he lugged his huge wicker basket up- or
downhill.

One day I arrived earlier than usual, paid the taxi and
window-shopped unhurriedly. It occurred to me that I
might try to interview one of the wares on display, so as
to give the setting of Jesus' story an interesting and
authentic touch. I stopped in front of one of the windows
and looked in. A Natasha was sitting sidelong on a barstool.
She was looking down; shoulder-length hair hid her face.
She was reading a book which lay open on her crossed
legs. There was something disturbing, I thought,
something incongruous about a prostitute reading a book.
How could one view them as objects to be used, then
discarded, if they read books? Did they have emotional
needs and social and cultural sensitivities?

It must have been a good book because the whore
remained oblivious to me for some minutes. I stared at her.
It struck me how beautiful she was. The red silk panties
with little white butterflies imprinted on them were cut
high so as to reveal the full length of her muscular legs
and hips. A low-cut bra of the same material displayed
more of her alabaster breasts than it covered. All at once I

had to repress a fiery urge to forget all about interviewing Jesus.

Just then she became aware of my presence, and turned to look. Her hair fell back to reveal an open, oval face and hazel eyes. She put her book to one side, laying it face down on a little table, and smiled. Her mouth opened and she ran her tongue slowly over her lips, moistening them, then she let it dart in and out of her mouth. I stood trans-fixed, like a mouse mesmerized by a cobra. Then, for a moment, I wanted to rough her up, to beat her, to mistreat her. What right had she to sit there and read while selling her body to every passerby? I felt a desperate urgency to find out what she was like, and to punish her for being as she was.

I looked at her girlish face, into the glimmering hazel eyes. I felt a hardness, a hatred, radiate from her and strike me through the glass like a physical blow. My mind flitted to Shimone: beautiful, yet with the same harshness in her eyes. I tore my eyes away and they lit on the cover of the book she was reading. To my surprise, it was in French. I looked back at the girl, nodded, and tried to smile. Then I felt silly. What would Hampar or Ali or Aziz or Misto or Shukru or Mahmut think if they saw me staring at a girl in a neon-framed window? She beckoned teasingly, but the spell was broken. I turned and headed for Jesus' place, walking rapidly up the hill. Shimone opened the door. Evidently she wasn't visiting her friends that evening.

I had a hard time concentrating on Jesus' narration. I let him ramble about how he left Abdul Kerim in the spring to make his way back to Amîd, and about the odd jobs he did to stay alive: carrying water for the baker or helping the butcher earned him a loaf of bread or a sheep's head or some cow intestines, which he cooked into soup in the cave he found for himself under the city walls.

My mind kept going back to the girl in the window. She was young, beautiful and cultured, yet hard, full of bitterness and hatred. I thought about Shimone. She had sat on the hard-backed chair at the foot of the bed for the duration of the interview. She too was young and beautiful, though not cultured — illiterate, no doubt. She rarely spoke a word, wrapping herself in a mysterious, detached, melancholy quietness. I wondered if the capacity for feeling had been snuffed out of her. Why was she full of bitterness and hatred? Is that what men did to women?

All at once I wanted to know more about this beautiful, hard, yet seemingly fragile girl, just as I had wanted to know more about the girl in the window. Who was she? Did she have no family other than the old man? What was her relationship to him anyway? What had happened to her parents? Were there no brothers or sisters or cousins or uncles or aunts? Or was she without family, as I was? Who would take care of her when the old man dies?

I became aware of an oppressive silence. The old man was dozing, and the tape recorder had clicked off. Shimone remained seated on her chair, staring impassively ahead of her. I suddenly had the same fiery urge I had felt earlier, but instead of wanting to hurt I wanted to be gentle; I wanted to caress her, to comfort her. I wanted her to be my friend and I wanted to buy her nice things.

"Shimone?" I said.

She turned her head toward me, seeing, yet her unfeeling eyes looked past me. I felt her willing me to leave.

"Shimone," I pleaded, then got stuck for words in a way I didn't with the secretaries of *The Morning*. "Shimone . . . "

"Please leave," she said, and her voice contained the same vehemence, the same bitterness, the same revulsion and the same hatred that had radiated from the girl in the window. It dawned on me that men had violated both of them. I left, feeling sordid.

∼∼∼

After the news and the weather, I reached for the remote and turned off the television. Father looked at me with raised eyebrows. "Aren't we going to watch the game?" he asked. He was lounging in his leather armchair, his feet on the coffee table, a glass of whisky in his hand. The housekeeper was doing the supper dishes in the kitchen.

"I was hoping you'd tell me what happened after 1846, after those Kurdish attacks on the Chaldeans and Nestorians," I said.

He rolled his eyes, put his glass down, yawned and stretched. "History repeated itself," he said. "You sure you want to miss the game?" he asked hopefully.

I smiled. Ever since I started visiting Jesus, Father and I seemed to be drawing closer together. There was a lightness, a buoyancy, about him I hadn't known before. He was almost funny, at times almost talkative. Although he had warned me repeatedly of the risks involved in my investigations, I sensed his support. My attempts to unearth the past seemed to have a therapeutic effect on him. It was as if I was doing something vicariously, doing something he wanted to do, but was incapable of carrying out.

I fished out the tape recorder, and he sighed in mock resignation.

"What happened after 1846?" I repeated the question when the tape started rolling.

He stared at the machine as he began to speak.

Pursued by the Past

My father's bare-bones explanations gave me enough information to know what to look for and where to find it. I approached my editor, told him in broad strokes what I was pursuing, and got his green light. *The Morning* then officially requested that one of their journalists be allowed access to the archives of the American Research Institute in Turkey. It came through in short order. I spent over a week reading through nineteenth century reports of the American Board of Commissioners for Foreign Missions, the mission agency which had operated on a large scale in Ottoman lands prior to World War I. A disturbing picture, part of which I described earlier, emerged. Worse was to come . . .

The missionaries were appalled by the ruthless persecution, the merciless cruelty, the rampage, rape and killing of the ethnic Christians during the 1840s, and moved to protect their flocks. They wrote letters to their respective boards and governments detailing the crimes they were witnessing, and demanded justice. And, of course, they rebuilt their schools, hospitals and printing presses.

From the Sultan's point of view the missionaries were a nuisance. Their human rights campaign stirred up a hornet's nest, the shock of which the Ottoman social fabric was simply too fragile to withstand. Furthermore, none of the parties understood the other; in fact, they didn't want to understand each other. Orthodox Christians, missionaries, and Muslims all needed to misunderstand each other in order to pursue their own agendas.

The Christians, particularly the Nestorians, were a small tribe in a hostile environment. They would embrace anyone who offered them a shield or a sword. More than anything, they wanted to throw off the yoke of Islamic and Kurdish oppression, and gain their independence. They were willing to join whichever group wielded the biggest club. At one point many of them even switched to the Russian Orthodox church, because they felt it offered more protection than the Protestants. When Russian rifles weren't forthcoming, and when Russia lost the war with Japan, they gave up on that idea. They told the missionaries that, in return for guns, they would re-Christianize the area, which they thought was the missionaries' goal as well. They simply thought of the missionaries as a powerful tribe who had come from afar to help them. They had no desire of becoming the vehicle through which the "gospel message" would reach the Kurds, something the missionaries failed to grasp.

The missionaries, on the other hand, never claimed to have political power or affiliation. Their goal was to establish the Kingdom of Christ in the hearts of men. They didn't want to understand the fact that the ancient churches wanted a political ally, not a spiritual revival. Neither did it occur to them that the historical churches had never agreed to the plans they had in mind for them. They simply couldn't understand that Christians didn't want Muslims in their churches, that, instead, they wanted them out of the land altogether. Nor did they understand the seditious nature of their own activities.

The missionaries' activities were considered seditious because graduates from their schools, virtually all Christian minorities, learned to read and think, and began to cherish democratic ideas. Remember, the Sultan ruled over numerous ethnic groups, and he couldn't have them all dreaming of their own little nation-states. Yet now, by courtesy of western missionaries, these people became aware of their distinctive cultures. They started producing an intelligentsia infected with western, liberal democratic ideas while the missionary printing presses promoted the standardization of languages, enabling minorities from all parts of the empire to communicate more easily with each other.

The missionary contribution to Armenian and Arab nationalism, in particular, was cultural. It inoculated these people against the government's attempt to homogenize the population — little wonder they came to be regarded as agents of foreign powers who sought to undermine its authority. The ancient churches, the Muslim majority, the central government and the missionary community were like four missiles which, once fired, can neither be recalled, nor change course. An explosion that would resolve the conflicting issues one way or another was merely a question of time.

In 1895 the Sultan unleashed the *Hamidiye*, his special Kurdish forces, against the Christian population. Once again, villages were destroyed, men were murdered and women raped. Once again the missionaries appealed to their respective embassies to intervene. This led, once again, to a cessation of activities, but only for the moment. Much worse was to come.

Those who led the Young Turk revolution of 1908 proclaimed pan-Turanism — the union of all Turkic people — as the official ideology. They promptly shut down all non-Turkish schools, associations and publications. They dreamt of a Turkish Empire stretching from the Balkans to the steppes of Central Asia. The problem was that their imaginary empire wasn't contiguous; it was divided by the Armenians, the Nestorians, and the Kurds, who occupied the area between Turkish Asia Minor and the Turkic states of Central Asia.

Under the cover of World War I, the revolutionary leaders implemented their "final solution" to that problem: they sought to annihilate the non-Turkic national entities. The Muslim Kurds were to be forcibly dispersed and assimilated, while the Christian nations, who were considered unassimilable, were to be exterminated. Regular Turkish troops aided by Kurdish militias decimated them. Close to a million Armenians and a quarter of a million Nestorians perished — by 1925 it was estimated that there were only about 10,000 Armenians left in the newly established republic. An entire civilization had vanished. War is a terrible thing, and the First World War was worse than any other conflict for the people of Anatolia. Those Christians who survived the genocide were scattered across the Middle East, across the world.

⁓⁓⁓

When the Research Institute closed for the night I'd take a taxi home and microwave the plate of food our cook had set aside for me. While I ate Father would wander into the kitchen, pull up a chair, ask what I'd discovered that day, and listen quietly. On the evening of my last day he looked at me across the table and asked quietly, "Would you like proof of our guilt?"

I looked at him questioningly.

"I mentioned earlier that my grandfather was in charge of the post office," he began. "When I was a boy he once showed me a huge bag of postage stamps. It was an amazing collection. There were stamps from Latin America, North America, from all over Europe, the Middle East. They were franked from Rio and Budapest, Marseilles and Los Angeles, Cairo, Aleppo, Baghdad, Damascus, Beirut, New York, Paris — from all over the world!" A haunted look clouded my father's eyes, a look such as I had never seen in him before. He went on, driven by some inner compulsion.

"I asked him where he had gotten them. He told me they were from Christians who had survived the death marches into the Syrian desert and were trying to trace members of their family. They were from husbands who were trying to find their wives, he said, and from fathers who were looking for their sons, and from mothers who had been separated from their daughters. None of the addresses were valid anymore, yet the government didn't allow the letters to be returned to the senders. So he kept the stamps. I asked him why he kept them. He said that they were his personal memorial to the evil his people had committed. They wouldn't allow him to forget, he said. I asked him why he didn't want to forget. He replied that great nations mustn't forget their past lest they be condemned to repeat its follies.

"Many years later, when I went to fetch Mother, I found that bag in the attic of our house in Amîd. I brought it back with me. It should be in that locked trunk in our store room in the basement."

I remembered the trunk Father referred to. I had been curious about it as a child. When I'd asked about it Father had said it contained old papers of his.

Father picked up his narrative. It was as though he was lancing an old, ugly, festering boil; it was as though he obtained some kind of perverse delight in seeing the puss squirt in every direction . . .

"Unspeakable atrocities were committed at that time, all in the name of holy war: a favourite trick, for instance, was to nail horseshoes to the feet of Christians, then order them to walk into the Syrian desert. As I mentioned before, your grandfather, my father, was one of the worst butchers, killing, torturing, and violating women." A twitch developed on my father's face, but he kept on speaking.

"Thousands of those who managed to escape joined the Russian army, and when it invaded the empire they wreaked a terrible revenge. They decimated the Turkish army and went on a rampage, killing nearly 800,000 Kurds.

"When the First World War ended in 1918, the Young Turk revolutionaries discovered that they had allied themselves to the wrong side. Their ephemeral empire was parceled out among the allies. The Arabs got their independence. At great cost Mustafa Kemal managed to salvage Asia Minor from the wreckage, to establish the modern republic. But, like the revolutionaries of 1908, the bedrock of his ideology was also race, so that even that great man continued to deny the past. As a result, the civilized world continues to loathe and distrust us. How can they trust a people that lie to itself about itself?

"That, my son, is our history. The sins of the fathers visit the children unto the third and fourth generation. We — you and I — have blood on our hands, much innocent blood." He fell silent for a moment, and then continued in a low voice. "Your great-grandfather was right. Unless we confess the sins of our fathers, they will haunt us forever," he said. "That is why I support your effort to uncover the past. We have to remember before we can forget and before we can be forgiven."

He lifted the glass to his lips and drained it. He looked exhausted, yet oddly happy, like the patient who has been released from the tyranny of a huge, inflammatory sore. The wound was still sensitive, but there was hope that healthy tissue would grow in its place.

～～～

After work the following day I went straight home. I made myself a mug of coffee, drank it, then headed for the basement.

It had been years since I'd gone down to the apartment's storage room. The odd time I needed my tool-chest, I only had to go as far as the little landing halfway down the staircase. I stepped over the tool chest, walked down the last five steps to the cement floor, then across the corridor to a steel door. The lock turned with difficulty, the door creaked when I pushed it open. I turned on the light as I stepped inside. The low-wattage light bulb revealed a rack of old clothes, mostly old-fashioned coats and dresses from my mother, and textbooks dating back to my father's university days. There was a wooden cupboard, and some shelves piled high with old magazines. My old ten-speed bicycle, its tires flat, was propped against the wall, next to an ancient red-plastic television. There was also a rusty shovel, a pickax, a garden hose, and bric-a-brac deemed too precious to throw out when Father re-decorated the house after mother moved out. The trunk stood against the back wall.

I moved towards it and walked into a spider's web; its tangle of silver strands and dead insects encased my face. I cursed, and tore the viscous filaments from my head and hair. Then I cleaned my glasses with my shirttail, and moved forward with care, holding an upright arm before my face.

The trunk had re-enforced steel corners; a padlock dangled from a U-shaped piece of metal. It was large, larger than I'd remembered. I pulled on the lid, but it wouldn't budge. I tugged at the padlock, but it was closed. The key had disappeared long ago. I took a second look at it. It was rusty. I jerked it again. Nothing happened. I thought for a moment, then headed for the cupboard.

The cupboard was stuffed with trays of old screws, nuts, bolts and nails, cans containing bits of coagulated paint, a bottle of turpentine and various rusty tools: a hammer with a broken handle, old screwdrivers, a saw with missing teeth, a wire-stripper. I found a crowbar on the bottom shelf.

The lock didn't offer much resistance. After the first jerk I felt some play, and a few more twists caused it to snap open. I lifted the lid and looked inside. I couldn't see much in the murky shade. I reached in, pulled a heavyish canvas duffel bag from the trunk, and set it on the floor beside me. It was large, standing higher than my waist when set upright. It smelled of mildew. I hauled it across the floor, into the light. Something in the old Ottoman script was printed on its side, along with the emblem of the post office. I had to smile: the emblem, two intertwined trumpets, hadn't changed in all those years. A moldy rope running through metal eyelets tied the old mailbag shut; it snapped in response to a few hard pulls. I reached into the bag and came up with a handful of old stamps.

The stamps were cut to little squares of yellowing paper that my great-grandfather had cut neatly from their envelopes. I reached in again, deeper this time, and came up with more stamps. Red ones with an icon and Magyar Posta printed on them, blue and brown ones with a map of South America saying Republica Argentina, purple ones with a farm girl carrying a basket on her head that said Poste Italiane, green ones with the profile of a woman wearing a laurel wreath with Republique Française printed on them.

I reached even deeper into the bag. More stamps. Belgie-Belgique, Hashemite Kingdom of Jordan, Republik Osterreich, Deutches Reich, Liban, Mexico, Canada, Nederland, España, Norge, Brasil, Sverige. I grabbed another handful: Helvetia, Bolivia, Posta Romana, Portugal, Misir-Egypt, Polska, Hellas . . .

There were thousands, no, tens of thousands, no, hundreds of thousands of stamps. Each represented a husband trying to find his wife, a father his sons, a mother her daughters. But the addresses were invalid, and the government didn't allow the letters to be returned to the senders. My great-grandfather didn't want to forget, he had said, because if we did we'd never learn from our errors. What had Father said? That we — he and I — have innocent blood on our hands. That unless we confess the sins of our fathers, they will haunt us forever. That we have to remember before we can forget and be forgiven . . .

I sat down on the basement floor, and the sack seemed to tower over me. I felt the guilt of history pressing down on me. I looked at the sack, and then I looked at my hands. They were dusty. I wished I could weep; I wanted to weep for those who wrote the letters, for those who had once lived at the invalid addresses, for my great-grandfather, the stamp collector, for my grandfather, the butcher, for my father who couldn't forget, for Jesus the Infidel who had survived, and for Shimone and the beautiful girl in the window who hated all men. I wanted to weep, but I hadn't wept since my parents' divorce. Although I willed them to, no tears came. The hardness of my heart frightened me.

CASSETTE #6, SIDE B:
THE TWINS MEET

"I remember that day as if it were a film playing before my eyes right now. I had run from Abdul Kerim over ten years earlier. I'd made my way to Amîd, where I'd found employment serving tea in Mahmut the Kurd's teahouse. I don't remember what day it was, or even what month. It was late summer during the Second World War. 1944. I remember every detail of that particular day — whatever day it was!

"The Khamsin was blowing from the Syrian desert. Sand invaded everything. It filtered through windows and doors, it cracked lips, abraded skin, frayed clothing and caked onto my mustache and eyelashes. It was morning, too early for customers. I was lying on my palette in the back room.

"A booming voice rang through the teahouse and I got up. A man, wearing the robe and black and white headdress of an Arab, was sitting by himself on one of the low stools. I walked to the samovar and asked him in Arabic if he wanted tea or something cold. From where I was sitting I couldn't see his face; it was hidden by the *kafiyeh*. He ordered tea, his booming voice reverberating around the empty room. I asked him whether he wanted it strong or weak; he wanted it strong. I filled the glass, dropped a teaspoon into it, put it on a saucer, grabbed a bowl of rock sugar from the shelf, and walked towards him.

At that moment the man threw his worry beads onto the table, flipped back the edge of his *kafiye* and turned up his face. Then time stood still. I remember stopping in mid-step, and I remember the Arab sucking in his breath. We stood there, staring at each other. It was as if we were looking at mirror images of ourselves. The hair, the eyes, the bushy eyebrows, the slope of the forehead, the cleft chin — that man was my double . . . , my twin!

"*'Isho . . . ? Isho, ha tat?'* The Arab asked falteringly in Aramaic. "Jesus . . . ? Jesus, is that you?"

"*'Yesh . . . Yeshua?'* I remember my voice cracking. "Joshua?"

"It had been nearly thirty years since I saw my twin brother disappearing in that column, and no one had called me Jesus in all that time; no one knew who I was, I barely knew myself!

"For ten years I had been an outcast, a person without a people. I had been unable to marry, because my own people, Amîd's small Chaldean remnant, would have nothing to do with a man without a clan, a Salih Aslan. And the real me — the me that knew the Aramaic Lord's Prayer — wouldn't marry anyone outside that community. How could one marry into a tribe which had raped and murdered one's loved ones and, but for the Lord's Prayer, had nearly snuffed out the memory of one's self as well?

"But here, standing as if by magic before me, stood my own blood brother! My twin, my own flesh, bone of my bone, the one with whom I had shared a womb, a breast, a cradle, a bed! We stared dumbly at each other, then Joshua reached out and touched my sleeve, as if to see whether or not I was real.

"Jesus . . . " he repeated.

"Yes," I said as much to myself as to him, "I am Jesus."

My eyes filled with water as I reached up and touched his cheek. He reached up too, and touched mine. Then we were embracing, weeping and talking all at the same time: he blubbered in Aramaic and Arabic, I in Turkish and Kurdish and broken Arabic, and we understood each other. We held each other close, then we held each other apart to better see each other, then we hugged and kissed again.

"I became aware that the Khamsin had intensified, blowing grit and sand against the window and billowing dirt through the crack under the door.

"'My brother,' I said, 'you blew in with the Khamsin. You must be thirsty.' My brother smiled. 'Never again will I curse the Khamsin,' he said. There was much emotion in his sonorous voice.

"The tea I had made for him lay spilled among fragments of glass on the floor, so I poured him another glass. Just then the door opened, letting in a cloud of sand along with several customers. I looked at my brother and saw him quietly wrap his *kafiye* around his face. Only his eyes remained visible. He looked at me and shook his head ever so slightly. I proceeded to serve the other customers. I don't remember anything about them, though I remember everything else about that day. I was standing at the samovar filling tea-glasses when I saw my brother put some money on the table, pick up his worry beads and amble towards the door. I watched him leave, bewildered. When he got to the door, he turned, pointed to his watch, and rapidly opened and closed his right hand twice. I nodded, and he stepped outside, the sepia storm swallowing him. I knew he would come for me at 10 PM that night.

"That was the longest day of my life. At times I was so excited I could barely contain myself. I wanted to run around the shop and tell everyone that I had found my family. I wanted to shout that it was true: if you waited long enough in Amîd you would eventually meet everyone you ever knew!

"Then I wondered if what had happened was real, if I wasn't imagining things, if I was living a dream. Mahmut, the Kurd who owned the teahouse, asked me if there was something wrong. I said no, but when I dropped two more glasses he got angry and shouted that if I didn't pay more attention he'd fire me. I didn't care if he fired me or not, so I just looked at him and smiled, and he told me to stop staring at him like an ass and to get back to work. Somehow I made it through that day, responding robot-like to cries of 'Salih, tea!'

"The teahouse always filled up after the supper hour, particularly on days when it had rained or snowed or if the Khamsin blew, because the men sought to escape wives who were irritable or talkative from having been cooped up all day. I wondered how I would get away, but my friend Hamdi showed up. I told him that I might have to slip out, and he promised to look after the teahouse for me.

"By evening the Khamsin had died down and the teahouse was full. Men were gathered around the little tables, slapping playing cards onto the green tablecloths, arranging the Rummicub tiles in sequential order, or just huddling together and discussing the war in Europe or new ideas for making money. Every time the door opened I jumped. Ten o'clock came and went, but my brother didn't show up. I became confused, and began wondering if I had hallucinated, if I had merely imagined embracing my brother that morning. It was close to eleven when the door opened again and an Arab, his head covered by his *kafiye*, stood briefly in the doorway, looked around, locked eyes with me, and disappeared. My heart leapt with joy. I raced around the teahouse getting rid of the glasses of tea on my tray, and told Hamdi I was on my way out. He nodded dozily and returned to his card game.

"It took my eyes a minute to adjust to the darkness, but then I saw the Arab, my brother, waiting for me at the top of the lane. I walked up to him. He put his arm through mine and we walked quietly in the darkness. I wondered where he was leading me. He took me along Yeni Kapi Street to Gazi Mustafa Kemal Boulevard, the wealthy district of the city, an area I rarely frequented. All the fancy hotels, cabarets and nightclubs were located there. We stopped in front of the Tigris Hotel, the poshest establishment of all, the one frequented by famous politicians, underworld figures and beautiful women. My brother unwrapped his *kafiye*, and told me to wrap it around my head instead. I did as he told me to and then, much to my surprise, we entered the Tigris. A man wearing an odd, striped uniform and a fez opened the door for us.

"I had stayed in numerous dilapidated inns and ramshackle caravansaries when I was on the road with Abdul Kerim, but I had never been inside a real hotel. The Tigris' lobby had plush, wine-red carpet on the floor, and walls of walnut paneling with etched mirrors built into them. A huge crystal chandelier hung from the ceiling. The place was stunning; I had never seen such opulence before. My brother walked to a desk which had another strangely uniformed man behind it who, when he saw my brother, nodded politely, then reached behind him to pull a key out

of a pigeon hole. The man barely glanced in my direction.
I noticed that he wasn't wearing a fez. My brother took the
key, and we walked towards a steel door set into the wall,
which a third uniformed man opened for us. The whole
thing looked a bit like Mahmut the Kurd's safe, only it was
much larger, large enough, in fact, for several people to
stand or squat in comfortably. My brother punched a
number on the wall, which I assumed was the safe's combi-
nation. I remember thinking that he was taking extraor-
dinary security measures. I was thunderstruck when the
whole contraption started moving upward ever so slowly
and very smoothly. It left the door behind and I could see
the wall rolling by. Every so often another steel door would
glide by. It was an eerie experience; my heart beat rapidly,
and my blood pulsated in my temples. But my brother
seemed to take it all in his stride, so I pretended to do so
as well. After passing three or four steel doors we came to
a halt before another such door, which opened of its own
accord. I was most relieved to get out of that moving safe
and put my feet on firm ground again.

"My brother led the way down the hall to a normal,
wooden door, opened it and waved me in. I entered a room
with two proper beds, bedside tables, two chairs, and a
cupboard. Off to one side were a private toilet, shower and
sink. I was overwhelmed by the luxury of the place.

"'My brother, my long-lost, my dearly beloved Jesus,' my
brother said as he turned to me. 'Take that *kafiye* off so I
can look at you again. God is great.' He hugged me, and I
hugged him again and again, and we kissed and wept
together.

"We sat up all that night and talked. I told him about
Abdul Kerim and Mother Ayshe, about my nightmares,

about travelling all over Kurdistan as Abdul's helper, about coming to Amîd, about leaving Abdul Kerim because I was really Jesus, son of Joseph, and not Salih, son of Abdul Kerim, about not being accepted by any community, about living in the cave outside the city walls, and about working for Mahmut the Kurd.

"Then my brother told me of all that had befallen him, and such of the family as had survived. He told how the Turkish soldiers had made them walk for days. There was harshness in his voice as he spoke of those times. He told how cousins and aunts and uncles died along the way, and how the soldiers had pushed the rest of them forward, without letting them bury their dead He said that our little sister Meryem died on that march, and that the chief soldier took our older sister Hanbak away, and that they never saw her again, either dead or alive. He shared how the soldiers disappeared one night, how they managed to stumble through the desert until they got to Qamishli, where American missionaries had built a tent city for the refugees. My brother described how twelve of them lived in a tent in the desert for years, living off American handouts. He told me he'd often thought of me, knowing with a knowledge that came from deep within his heart that I wasn't dead. They'd lived in fear of marauding Turkish and Kurdish irregulars who raided the vicinity of the camp. He and our uncles got a job stretching barbed wire from the eastern to the western horizon, and then, after the wire was laid, they were told that they were safe from the Turks and Kurds now. The empire was gone, and the wire was the boundary between two new countries, the Republic of Turkey on the far side and the Kingdom of Syria on their side. They were told that the war was over, and that they could leave the camps.

"'But where could we go?' my brother asked rhetorically. 'Our village lay on the other side of the wire. What had happened to it? What had become of our fields, our houses, our cattle, our church? It was decided that Uncle Budrus would go and take a look. We cut a hole in the wire and he crawled through it to the other side one night. He was gone for nearly a month. We wondered if he had been killed, but he eventually came back. He reported that plains Kurds had moved into our village and had taken everything that was ours. Uncle Budrus had also travelled to Mardin and Amîd to see if any of our relatives were alive there. In Mardin he did find some family, some distant relatives, people I didn't know from a neighbouring village. They, too, had lost their farms and their livestock, he said, and survived by running a little grocery store.

"Uncle Budrus spent some time helping them, learning all he could about running a business. He learned all about the prices of things there in Mardin before returning back to the camp. After he came back, the family had a long, all-night parley. You see, Uncle Budrus had discovered that some things they were selling in Mardin were much cheaper on our side of the wire, while other things were much more expensive. We pooled what little money we had earned from helping to string the wire fence, and from other odd jobs. Uncle Budrus spent it on those things he said were cheap in Syria, like lard and sugar. Medicine was also expensive in Turkey, he said, so all of us feigned sickness. We went to the dispensary complaining of one thing or another — diarrhea, headaches, stomach cramps — and the missionaries gave us medicine. One night Uncle

Budrus crawled through the wire again, this time carrying a large bag of goods. He went straight to our distant relatives in Mardin, who bought everything from him. With the money he earned he bought bolts of cloth, which he somehow managed to haul back to Syria. We sold the cloth to the Kurds and Arabs of the surrounding villages, and made a killing. Then we bought more lard and sugar and got more medicine. On his next trip Uncle Budrus took me along. He needed someone to help him carry all our stuff.

"'We are rich now,' my brother said. "We take guns, ammunition, radios — anything that fetches a good price in Turkey. We even hauled an anti-aircraft gun across the border once and sold it to a Kurdish agha. We return with tobacco, car parts, anything. Uncle Budrus died some years ago, when they started laying mines between the barbed wire fences. I took over the business, and have been expanding it ever since.'"

My Suspicion is Confirmed

Moonlight has a way of transforming the ugly into the sublime. God gave the long, glimmering, white beams playing hide-and-seek with the clouds an uncanny ability to cover crumbling squalor and highlight basic forms: square, round, angular. Its low, inconsistent intensity imparts a restfulness, a stillness, to drab gutters and drainpipes, to uneven pavements and cobblestone alleys which sunlight denies it.

I wandered slowly down the incline, toward the red lights, where I hoped to find a taxi. It was late; the streets were deserted. Life with all of its songs, fights, laughter, noise, smiles, cries and violence took place behind closed doors at this time of the night. I passed by the store of Andreas Stephanopolis. A ray of light escaped from under the roll-down shutters, and I could hear his cracked voice droning a Greek hymn. At that hour Andreas Stephanopolis gave God what he thought was His due. Sometimes he'd murmur through the entire orthodox mass, ending in the Lord's Prayer in Greek.

Further down I heard a young mother singing a lullaby to a child. The child refused to sleep, and the mother started over again. The child wept, so the mother beat it, and the father cursed them both. Another day in the life of Aziz the Porter was drawing to a close. I could hear Aziz groan, his back burning where the wicker baskets he carried up and down the hill had dug into it. His wife pulled out her breast and shoved it into the little one's face. But how much milk can bread and beans produce?

Down the street a father had returned home drunk and was beating those in the house in sequence of age. The wife and daughters were screaming, the little ones crying, the man swore and shouted.

Andreas Stephanopolis' cracked voice, babies and children crying, girls and women screaming, men cursing or snoring. The sounds mixed to produce a misbegotten symphony in my head.

I couldn't get Jesus out of my mind. "Hanbak," he had said. Now I knew for certain what I had suspected since my third or fourth visit. It had been his eyes, the slope of his forehead, his cleft chin, that had made me suspicious.

We knew my grandmother by her Turkish name, Hanim, but Mr. Mehmet Shimshek had said she was really a Chaldean woman named Hanbak. Jesus and I were relatives! He was my grandmother's younger brother, my father's uncle! The revelation seemed so implausible, so far-out, and yet so possible, so . . . expected. I felt as though I was fulfilling an appointment with destiny; the feeling left me flushed and elated, yet apprehensive, edgy. I had to suppress an urge to scream and shout, to love, to inflict pain, to go to the edge, to self-destruct!

Jesus had gone on to tell how he and his brother had slept late the next morning, of his astonishment when his brother ordered breakfast from the black box on the bedside table and how a man in uniform had delivered it to their room a little later. He had told his brother that he had to get back to Mahmut the Kurd or he'd be fired, because he'd broken three glasses the previous day, and of how his brother had laughed and said he needn't ever go back to Mahmut the Kurd again. He told me how they'd wept with happiness again, and then, as if reliving the event all over, Jesus had starting weeping before me, his blotched, old head bobbing up and down, the tears rolling down his wrinkled face and staining his vest. At that point Shimone, home that night, had nodded curtly, indicating that it was time for me to go.

When I got down the hill a taxi was waiting, but I didn't hail it. I kept walking until I got to the window that belonged to the beautiful Slavic girl who read French books. She wasn't there, but a book with Cyrillic characters lay closed on the stool, a tasseled bookmark protruding from one end. I crossed the street and squatted against a wall, half-hidden by a garbage bin. For about ten minutes I gazed blindly into the pulsating neon light splitting the night. Then a fat, swarthy, wealthy looking, middle-aged man stepped out of the doorway next to the window and flagged down a cruising cab. The girl appeared in the window wearing a peach-coloured negligee. She proceeded to brush her hair in long, smooth strokes. She put her face close to the mirror and adjusted her lipstick, picked the book off her stool, sat down, opened it and began to read. She was beautiful, innocent, dangerous, full of malevolence yet offering brief respites of ecstasy. I wanted her; I didn't care how many fat, swarthy, middle-aged men had preceded me; I wanted to enter fully into this ugly yet attractive, this repulsive yet fascinating world. If I did, I might understand Jesus the Infidel, Jesus my relative better. I stood up from behind the garbage bin and crossed the road. She looked up, saw me coming, put the tasseled bookmarker in place and closed the book.

I returned home late that night, feeling wasted, empty, vile.

～～～

I was unable to see Jesus in the same light again; he was, after all, my relative, my father's uncle. I didn't tell him, but I told Father.

"I told you that you'd bring the house down. This is only the beginning. The worst is yet to come."

I asked him what he meant and he told me not to be naive. The General didn't want people delving into the past or showing an interest in minorities. The Hill is crawling with secret police, he added, and they know only too well what you're up to.

I asked him if he didn't think we had a moral obligation toward Jesus; he told me he wasn't my conscience. I had unearthed those people, he said, and I had to decide whether I'd re-bury them or not. I asked him what he thought I should do. He told me I was free to do as I wanted.

"In that case, I'm going to pursue this story to the end," I said. He rewarded me with one of his enigmatic smiles.

CASSETTE #7, SIDE A:
THE BROTHERS MAKE PLANS

"For the next week my brother and I lived in the Tigris hotel. During the day, and sometimes late at night, Joshua would leave on mysterious errands while I showered, slept, went to the barber, bought myself new clothes, and had kebabs and mezzes delivered to our room. For some days I thought I had died and gone to heaven.

"There was, however, something which troubled me about my brother's business. The fact that it was illegal didn't bother me — the laws of a state that sought to exterminate my people meant as little to me as it did to him. The thing that did worry me was Joshua's contact with Enis the One-eyed, the man my brother had been hoping to contact when he walked unexpectedly into Mahmut the Kurd's teahouse.

"One evening we went for supper to an exclusive fish restaurant overlooking the river. Here, away from the Tigris hotel, away from the east end, in the privacy of the posh restaurant, Joshua felt free to uncover his face in my company. I was, in any case, barely recognizable in my new cap, shirt, vest, suit jacket and baggy trousers. I was trying to twirl my bone worry beads with the fingers of one hand, and hold a demi-cup of Turkish coffee by its dainty ear in the other. *Mezze*, fish, mixed salad and fruit had come and gone. The fawning waiter had cleared the dishes. The lute players and the belly dancer were taking a break. All was quiet. I put the coffee cup down and leaned across the table.

"'My brother,' I said. 'I have heard about that man, Enis the One-eyed, whom you are visiting. He is very rich, very dangerous. He controls the east end. Everyone fears him.'

"'Tell me what you know about him.'

"'Even the police fear him. He controls a gang of thugs who carry out his orders. Every business in the east end must pay him money. One of his men comes to Mahmut the Kurd's teahouse every month, and he pays them.'

"'Would you recognize Enis the One-eyed or his men?'

"'I have never seen Enis the One-eyed. I would recognize the man who collects the money from Mahmut the Kurd.'

"'Would they recognize you?'

"'I merely serve tea, my brother. I don't suppose they'd recognize me now,' I smiled and stroked the lapel of my new suit. 'But if you cross Enis the One-eyed, or if he distrusts you, your battered body will end up floating face down in the river or smeared over the cobblestones. My brother, what do you need him for, that you seek him out?'

"Joshua sipped his coffee and said nothing for some minutes. Then he put the cup down, planted his elbows on the table and rested his chin on his clasped hands. 'The man who ran our affairs in Turkey, the son of Uncle Budrus' original contact in Mardin, was arrested last month. I'm looking for someone else to market our stuff,' he said quietly.

"'Is there no one to take over from the arrested man?'

"'We think someone from inside their network gave him away. We have decided to cut all contact with them. We don't know whom of that clan we can trust any more, and we don't have other connections. We are small fry, my brother, and we're happy to stay that way. We wanted to keep the business entirely within the family. But men like your Enis the One-eyed want us to expand before he is prepared to commit his resources. Enis the One-eyed wants us to specialize in the dried powder of the opium poppy . . . '

"We sat in silence, sipping coffee and gazing into the darkly flowing water beneath, and at the moon-tinted clouds above.

"'My brother,' I spoke up. 'I can pull teeth and I can run a teahouse. I know Kurdistan well, having travelled everywhere with Abdul Kerim. Could you not teach me to market your goods?'

"'Enis the One-eyed and some of his men have seen my face,' Joshua spoke slowly and with a frown. 'If I were to set you up in business here he would send his men to extort money from you, and they would immediately recognize you as my twin brother.'

"'I am Jesus, son of Joseph, but only you know that,' I said thoughtfully. 'I could go elsewhere and remain Salih Aslan, son of Abdul Kerim Aslan. You provide me with goods that I can sell to the villagers and I can take care of the rest. My brother, the business would stay in the family and you wouldn't have to deal in the dried powder of the opium poppy. Could I not move to Mardin?'

"'Mardin is also impossible. Whoever turned our friends there over to the police will know me as well. Neither you nor I can be seen there. I came looking for new contacts here in Amîd because I didn't think anyone here knew me.'

"'God is merciful. The arrest of your friend led you to me.'

"'Amen,' Joshua said with fervor. 'My brother, your idea is good,' he added. 'You would have to move somewhere where no one knows either of us. It must be a place not too far west, as we don't know the border crossings there like we know them here. Nor must we be caught competing with the gangs who operate there. That would be our undoing. Do you still have contact with your people in the mountains?'

"'I try to send some money to Abdul Kerim and Mother Ayshe when I can. They saved my life, and I feel responsible for them. Abdul Kerim is getting old, too old to travel the mountains. Reward is a fine young man. He tried to take over from his father, but the government is clamping down on unlicensed practitioners. But they are known and loved in many villages.' Whenever I thought of Abdul Kerim a feeling of nostalgia filled me. Those years on the road with Abdul the Toothdoctor were some of my most precious memories. Although I had left Abdul Kerim and Mother Ayshe, I had not forgotten them.

"Joshua appeared very moved as he listened to me. He reached across the table and took hold of my hand and squeezed it, and we smiled over the table and looked into the other's eyes.

"'Urfa,' I said slowly. 'Is Urfa not possible?'

"'Urfa . . . ' Joshua's voice trailed off as he pondered the thought.

"'I've never been there, but I've heard about it,' I continued. 'Its southwest of here, close to the border. Kurdish and Arab aghas own the land all around it, but the town is a mixture of Turks, Arabs, Kurds and some

Christians. Also, people from all over the country, even from Iran and from Arab countries, go there on pilgrimage. It is a very ancient city. Terah, the prophet Abraham's father, and the prophet Job, lie buried there.'

"Joshua looked thoughtful. 'Do you think you can do it, my brother?' he asked.

"'What is the difference between running a teahouse and any other kind of business? Mahmut the Kurd buys big bags of tea cheaply and sells it one glass at a time. My brother, suppose you open a store in Urfa, a real store, which I will run for you like I ran Mahmut the Kurd's teahouse. You provide me with cheap things from Syria, which I will sell for you in the store along with other, local produce. Reward could peddle our merchandise in small quantities in the villages. You would buy other things cheaply from our own store, and sell them in Syria. The business would stay entirely in the family and you wouldn't have to mess with Enis the One-eyed or with the powder from the opium poppy!' My voice was animated, and my hands moved excitedly as I spoke.

"Joshua's face slowly turned into a wide grin. 'It was God who directed me to the teahouse of Mahmut the Kurd,' he said. 'Tomorrow we leave for Urfa . . . '"

∽∾∽

Jesus and I were destined to visit Urfa half a century after he first set up shop there. Although my first glimpse of the place occurred in the 1990s and not in the 1940s, it was easy to imagine what it must have been like when the two brothers travelled there in the last year of the Second World War. Time there moves at a mere fraction of the speed it does elsewhere.

Urfa is an unusual place. True, every city, every town in the Middle East has its own flavour, its own ambiance, but Urfa, Edessa of old, is in a category by itself. The dark and mysterious processes that govern history dictated that this blank spot sizzling in the sun on the northern flank of the Mesopotamian plateau would be the focal point of countless battles. Here armies from Carchemish and Hatushash, from Cairo, Nineveh and Babylon, from Macedonia and Csestiphon, from Rome and Persipolis, from Constantinople, Damascus and Baghdad, from Ankara and Paris soaked the arid soil with their blood. Ancient Harran lies just southward, the mighty stone heads of Antiochus Epiphanes and his fellow gods lie in a jumbled heap in the mountains to the north.

A mighty fortress sporting two huge columns, jointly known as Nimrod's throne, overlooks the city from the top of a towering rock pillar. In its shade, near the cave said to be the prophet Abraham's birthplace, are pools full of sacred carp — sacred because their forefathers were once the woodpile used in Abraham's funeral pyre. Nimrod took offense at Abraham's iconoclastic zeal, and had him arrested and immolated. At the last moment, however, God intervened, turning the fire into water, and the wood into fish and thus rescued His man. Cool, shady parks surrounding the pools boast gnarled eucalyptus trees under which one can escape the sun, drink tea, and feed sunflower seeds to the fish. The ancient Rizvaniye and Abdurrahman Mosques flank the park.

Just east of the pool, on the far side of yet another mosque, the one that entombs the cave where Abraham was born, lies Urfa's labyrinthine covered market. I remember Jesus' excitement as I pushed his wheelchair through the sprawling area. He directed me this way and that, until we came out the *souq*'s other end, near the Great Mosque on Divan Boulevard. There he led me to a large stone building, four floors high, which housed a carpet business.

"This," he said, "used to be our store."

"All four floors?" I asked jokingly.

"Yes, youngster." His scrawny chest puffed up proudly. "Our goods were divided into different departments. I had between sixteen and twenty people-working for me.

I looked at the large, piebald, flagstoned structure with its vaulted portico supported by Arab style horse-shoe arches, and then I looked down in amazement at the old man I had been pushing in the wheelchair. Once upon a time this must have been the largest store in town! The old man had pioneered the department store phenomena in the region.

"When I met my brother it had been more than a decade since I left Abdul Kerim, Mother Ayshe and Reward. Although I had not visited Bezal in that time, I had found Abdul Kerim about two years after I'd run away from him.

"You see, I was the loneliest man in Amîd at that time, for I belonged to no clan, no tribe. So, about eight months after I'd run away, I started dropping by the inn where Abdul lodged whenever he came to Amîd to buy gold. I longed to run into my savior, the only father I really knew, my only teacher. I pined for him, his fellowship, the freedom of the trail, and I desperately missed Bezal, Mother Ayshe, Reward . . .

"And one day there he was, an aging man sitting at a low table reading an outdated magazine. I walked slowly, hesitantly towards him, my heart beating in my throat. He looked up and saw me.

"I rushed forward, grabbed his right hand, kissed it and raised it to my forehead to show respect, but Abdul pulled away, stepped back and, with silent, brooding eyes, stared at me for a long, awkward eternity. I accepted his gaze unflinchingly, because I was not ashamed, though I feared that he would renounce me. I saw that he had suffered, that he was perplexed, dismayed; only then did I appreciate the depth of his love for me, a love I had cruelly spurned.

"Praise God, it was not his nature to spurn. He bade me sit down and, in a voice trembling with emotion he said, 'Tell me everything, my son.'

"We sat on low stools drinking tea in the inn's courtyard, and I told Abdul Kerim why I had left. He listened silently as I spoke.

"'Son,' he said finally, 'If you had been our own flesh and blood, Mother Ayshe and I would have had reason for resentment. But you are someone else's flesh and blood, so we have no rightful hold on you. I pray that God will lead you to your own people, and when he does, give yourself wholeheartedly to them. That is the way of God.'

"I never felt so lonely, so broken, as when I said goodbye to the faithful old man that evening . . .

"After that Abdul Kerim looked me up whenever he was in town. But the visits became more and more infrequent, then ceased altogether. That was when I started sending money to the village whenever I was in a position to do so.

"The journey back to the village was much easier in the spring of 1945 than it had been before the war. A bus ran all the way from Amîd over the mountains to Hakkari. I got off when it reached Beytushebab in the evening, and spent the night in the ramshackle inn there. I got up early the next morning and started hiking upstream along the path beside the creek. Following its curves I made my way over rounding boulders and rambling clumps of rhododendron thickets until I entered a long canyon. Below me a wild little stream stormed over rocks and boulders, above me clouds glowed in the luminous pink light of morning, and around me the sun drew the silver veil clinging to the slopes to itself. I found myself walking on a carpet of early spring flowers. The air, still crisp from the night-frost, circulated in gentle currents against the sun-warmed hillsides.

"By noon I was walking through the hamlet that once featured so prominently in my nightmares. I ignored the menacing dogs, the brown-eyed, barefooted children scurrying after me, and the men and women who looked curiously at the well-dressed man striding through their village.

"I looked at the hills on my right, and saw the brush-covered rock where I had hidden when the soldiers rounded up my loved ones. It seemed so near. The church still had the minaret perched on the bell-tower. Mother used to light candles in that building, kneel at the ornately carved, stone altar and say the Lord's Prayer, while Father Sabri swung his incense burner singing *'kidis, kidis, kidis'*, holy, holy, holy. There, in the courtyard in front of the church, was the place where the soldiers had lined everyone up before they marched them away. The adobe building to the left was the house in which the soldiers had raped my mother and sister, the house in which I was born.

"A middle-aged Kurd wearing a tasseled white and black turban, an embroidered vest, baggy trousers of homespun, grey wool and a cummerbund knotted intricately was sitting in the doorway of our ancestral home. The man stood up when he saw me coming.

"*'Tu bi selamet hatin,'* he said. 'You have come in peace.'

"'I have come in peace.'

"*'Hat, çaya me waxwe.'* 'Come, drink our tea.'

"'Thank you, but I must reach Bezal before evening.' I wanted very much to enter the old homestead.

"'Then there is time for tea. The road to Bezal is not long.'

"'It is long, my father,' I replied, and hope surged in me.

"'I will loan you my donkey. You will arrive early.'

"I entered my parental home. My host offered me the seat of honour on the mattress. A woman wearing fortress-like layers of multicoloured clothing — pantaloons, slips, dresses, an overcoat, a vest and several scarves — appeared holding a bottle of cologne. She sprinkled some into my cupped palms. I rubbed my hands together, inhaled the fragrance and patted some onto my neck, face and hair. The woman disappeared into the back room, to reappear some minutes later with a bowl of water. She knelt down and washed my feet.

"'You have business in Bezal?' the man asked.

"'I am from Bezal. I am Salih, the son of Abdul the tooth-doctor,' I replied.

"'Abdul Kerim is an honorable man, as is his son Reward,' the man said, his voice betraying none of his surprise.

"'I haven't been home in many years. I travelled much with Abdul Kerim when I was a boy. Then I stayed behind in Amîd. I now own a store and have come to help Abdul Kerim and Mother Ayshe in their old age.'

"'I remember you, my son. You were the boy with the chestnut donkey who used to accompany Abdul. God have mercy on you, my son.'

"'And on you.'

"The woman dried my feet with a towel, got up, and went into the back room. She returned shortly to place small bowls filled with pistachio nuts, salted pumpkin and melon seeds, almonds and dried fruit before me, as well as an empty dish for nutshells and cigarette ash.

"The old Kurd and I talked about political developments in Ankara and Amîd, and the needs of the people of Kurdistan. The woman handed her husband a tray with two glasses of tea and a bowl of rock-sugar on it. He handed me one of the glasses, and put the sugar bowl between us. We each put a lump of sugar between our lower teeth and lip and sipped tea through it. It was good quality, Iraqi tea. Snacks and tea relax people and thus stimulate good conversation.

"I had to suppress the urge to look around me — overt curiosity is dishonorable — yet managed to steal glances in every direction. I recognized the place where mother used to cook, where father used to sit and carve wooden spoons, and where Joshua and I once wrestled during the long winter days. Some things were different. There were now two windowpanes to let light into the room, and a stone chimney had been punched through the roof. I discovered that I could look at these things without rancour, without hate. The night had passed, I thought. Dawn had broken. We had lost our land, but I was re-united with my family, with my own people. I was content.

"The Kurd lent me his donkey and I rode it to Bezal. As I approached the village that evening I noticed a man wearing light-coloured clothes and a wire veil moving slowly among some beehives in the field to my right. The man looked curiously in my direction, then started running clumsily towards me, waving his arms and ripping the protective cover from his head. I slipped from the animal and ran toward Abdul Kerim, meeting him, hugging him, squeezing him tightly to myself in the middle of the field.

"Abdul Kerim had grown old. His hair was silver-grey, his skin wrinkled as parchment, and there was a cloudy ring around the cornea of his eyes. But he still had a clarity of mind, a brightness of spirit, a graciousness of character that touched me deeply.

"Mother Ayshe lay buried in the hill above the house. She had passed away eight months earlier. Reward was eking out a living for the two of them by farming the land Abdul Kerim had bought with his life's savings.

"Time, in Kurdistan, is measured by the season, not the hour. In the following days and weeks I cut firewood, helped Reward in the fields and Abdul with the beehives. The other villagers viewed me with suspicion, and I tried to avoid them. Twice I walked over the pass to visit the friendly Kurd who lived in my parents' home. When I finally departed, all the necessary arrangements were in place. Joshua and I could take the next step."

CASSETTE #8, SIDE A:
JESUS' WEDDING

"Chaldean weddings, including mine, were celebrated in style. We incorporated all the traditional rites and rituals into our ceremony.

"On the first day the women came to inspect my bride's trousseau, the doilies, tablecloths, pillow covers, bedspreads, embroidered dresses, nightgowns and numerous other items she had made herself. They admired her handiwork, then ululated with happiness, their shrill *lululululu* reaching the teahouse, where the men had congregated.

"The next day my bride, wearing multiple layers of light-coloured gauze, was taken to the public bath. An old crone banged a tambourine to warn the men to look the other way as the party passed by them on its way to the bathhouse. There my bride's clothes were removed one layer at a time until she stood naked before Joshua's wife, who stood in for our murdered mother. Joshua's wife carefully inspected my bride's body to ensure that it was unblemished. After she passed that test, the women bathed her and, using wax, removed every vestige of body hair, excepting the luxuriant black mass tumbling from her head. They massaged her from tip to toe with an oily cream until she was soft and supple, then they braided white beads into her locks.

"On the third day Joshua and his wife, and their sons and daughters and friends, made their way to my bride's house. They were served various dishes my bride herself had prepared. Joshua said that the pilav was too salty and the meat too tough, but that the bride was beautiful. They presented a dowry of gold jewelry to my bride's mother, and counted out much money to her father. Then the truck with our furnishings arrived. It was a magnificent trousseau, such as had never been seen before: new clothing, a sewing machine, a cooking stove, pots, pans, cups, wardrobes, furniture, beds, mattresses, quilts, blankets, and sacks of food. The bride's family was overwhelmed, and knew with a surety that the groom could provide for his wife.

"The next morning, on the fourth day, my bride's relatives and friends came to bid farewell. As all brides do, my bride wept loudly as she kissed them. Later that same day Joshua, his wife, and their entourage came to take her from her parental home and she left with them, accompanied by her older, married sister and her best friend. They came to help her prepare the pre-wedding party that evening, at which time her hands and those of her guests would be dyed crimson with henna.

"On the morning of the fifth day the bride's sister and her best friend helped my bride dress for the wedding celebration. They walked her to church, where she saw me, her husband to be, for the first time. She was not surprised, as people had told her that I was a mirror image of her Uncle Joshua.

"After the priest led us through our marriage vows, I lifted the red veil and saw the oval face of a fourteen-year-old girl. She had large black eyes and a smooth, olive skin.

She glanced up at me briefly and then looked down demurely, and I knew that Joshua and his wife had chosen well. I knew that my bride would please me.

"After the conclusion of the church ceremony, the party began. It lasted for another three days. The guests wore their best clothes, and presented gold to the bride or pinned money onto her dress. Hired musicians played the oboe, the drum, the saz and the lute. There were mountains of food: lamb, chicken, rice, vegetable stew and bread washed down with yogurt drink and tea. My bride sat with downcast eyes next to me, showing the appropriate amount of embarrassment at being the centre of so much attention, thus revealing her good breeding. Unmarried young men tried to catch the eye of future spouses, by jumping onto the back of an old truck and driving wildly all over town waving flags, banging drums and playing the *zurna*.

"After the ceremony my bride and I were led to Joshua's house, where we consummated our marriage. The old crone, the bride's grandmother, received the bloodied bed sheet, proof of her granddaughter's virginity, with joy. She carried the good news back to her family, who had been absent from all the celebrations to show their grief at losing a family member. The men and boys of that household shouted and the women ululated upon receipt of the bed sheet, because the family's honour had been maintained.

"After the wedding my bride and I observed the "*çel*", the week long period of seclusion which follows the wedding night. It is a time when new couples are particularly vulnerable to evil. We stayed indoors and accepted no visitors. After the *çel*, my bride returned to her parents' house carrying gifts I had given her to give to them, to show them how pleased I was with their daughter. She stayed with her own family for a week to entertain old friends and distribute gifts. Then Joshua and I came to take her away for good.

"Joshua, my bride, and the truck carrying the enormous load of furnishings crossed the border without trouble. Their papers were in order; the right palms had been greased. I quietly slipped across no man's land later that night, and we met the following day at the appointed place. Joshua drove us to Urfa.

"Most of the spectacular trousseau was earmarked as stock for the new store. Our business got off to a good start."

Jesus Forces My Hand

I connected my cell phone to the laptop, e-mailed the report to my editor, put the computer away and signaled the waiter.

"Another coffee, please."

"Coming, sir."

It was dusk. The night promised to be as sultry as the day had been. The riot had been another lethargic affair, a token show. The rioters were gone, and the police were filing neatly into their white and black busses. There had been few arrests, and no brawls worth filming. The cameramen had packed up their gear and left disappointed.

Crowds once again milled across the square. Locals strode homeward after a day's work, wandering tourists drifted in and out of the cafés and restaurants along the boulevard, and students, emanating the confident enthusiasm of youth, were scattered in little groups around the tea garden and conversed animatedly about the issues of the day. A disconsolate ballad about someone who had been unjustly imprisoned drifted from the speakers hanging among the branches of the great sycamore trees. Someone switched on the lights. The coffee came; I stirred it absentmindedly.

Over breakfast the previous morning I had told Father that I wanted to go to Amîd.

"Why?" he had asked.

157

"For the same reason you went when you were my age,"
I replied. "We have family there — uncles, aunts, cousins,
nieces, nephews. I want to meet them."

"They are half-uncles, aunts, cousins, nieces and
nephews."

"Let's not get technical. They are family! You know,
Jesus clung to his identity even when he thought he was
the only one left. That's loyalty! What family do we relate
to? None. What family do I have? You and mother, and she's
preoccupied with her lovers. But now I don't just have
you," I'd added quietly. "I have Jesus, too. Knowing him,
listening to him, has enriched me more than he — or you
— can imagine. I want to find out who else is related to
me."

My father had smiled his enigmatic smile. "Don't get
hot under the collar," he said. "Go ahead. I wouldn't want
to deprive you. I'll give you some addresses. That way you
don't need to bother our friend, Mr. Mehmet Shimshek."

I had looked at him sharply, but he'd merely popped
another olive into his mouth, got up from the table,
grabbed his briefcase, and patted me on the head as he
walked out the door.

That afternoon I had had another interview with Jesus.
He was long-winded, talking about how their business had
an edge on competition because of the goods coming
across the border, and how Reward peddled their stuff in
the mountain villages, eventually becoming a respected
wholesaler in his own right.

The 1950s and 1960s were the glory decades of his life.
Meryem, his bride, bore him two sons, Metin and Misak,
and a daughter, Mary, the apple of his eye. After she was
born they moved from the apartment above the store to a

house with a garden. Somehow, for most of that turbulent period, they managed to stay aloof of the convolutions that seized our country at that time.

～～～

The '50s and '60s saw rapid change worldwide, but the nature of the change between the West and Anatolia was totally different. In the West scientific and technological advancements put men on the moon, medical progress saved numerous lives, Blacks fought for and obtained civil rights, the Cold War contained Communism, the economy expanded rapidly, and people drifted from the cities to the suburbs. The '50s and '60s transformed our country as well, though in a totally different direction. State radio and official education mocked the sheiks and aghas, and new ideologies percolating through the area challenged traditional devotion to the tribe. Conflicting calls for loyalty to the State, or to the Islamic community, or to the working class, or to the Kurdish nation, produced a ferment of political debate and action. Peasants revolted against aghas, refused to pay tribute, and defended themselves with firearms. Land reforms turned sharecroppers into landless day labourers or into heavily indebted owners of small, untenable plots. Entrepreneurs bought the land from the small landowners, and introduced mechanized farming techniques. Former farmers, peasants and day labourers drifted into the cities to become the nucleus of an embittered urban proletariat. The disaffected also crossed the borders and fought in the wars of liberation of neighbouring countries; those who survived returned home with more outspoken political ideas and a greater awareness of the oppression their own people faced. Nationalist notions cross-pollinated with radical socialism to produce a heady potent for an impoverished, disinherited people. Unemployed youths obtained guns, headed for the mountains and formed armed bands. First they raided isolated farms, then villages, and eventually they organized night raids on towns. They even attacked army convoys snaking through the narrow mountain passes.

Meanwhile, in the cities, idealistic students printed socialist and communist propaganda on cheap paper, and formed urban cells in the sprawling new slums. The charismatic rebel leader of a Marxist-Leninist-nationalist organization operating in the mountains made contact with these urban cell groups, and provided them with arms and money. By the early seventies the leader had marshaled such forces that he actually threatened the stability of the republic. Parliament divided into a plethora of factions: Fascist, Communist, Socialist, Islamist, Nationalist, Turanist, Kurdish, Kemalist, Leftist, Rightist, Centrist, each of which was, in turn, divided into pro-Western, pro-Soviet, and pro-non-aligned cabals. Coalition governments formed and fell in rapid succession, inflation spiraled. Surrounding nations saw their chance to destabilize the country further by supporting the rebels. The rebel leader soon controlled much of the countryside in the Southeast and, at night, the towns as well. His thugs extorted money from hapless businessmen. The army became restless as the country slid towards civil war . . .

∾∾∾

After my interview with Jesus I told him I wouldn't be coming for two or three weeks.

"I shall miss you," he said, and I knew he meant it. He enjoyed my visits; they broke his monotonous existence in that claustrophobic little room. "Where will you be going?" he asked.

"I am going to the South-East!" I said. "If I'm going to write intelligently about it I must see the place for myself. I want to see those mountains, those plains, those villages you have been describing. I want to walk through the warren of Amîd's Infidel Quarter and eat fish above the Tigris river . . . " I was leaning forward, collecting my recording equipment when suddenly Jesus' withered hands clasped my wrists.

"Take me along," he said, his voice urgent, fiery. I looked up in surprise and had to suppress an urge to laugh. But his eyes, as always strangely enlarged by the thick lenses, pled with me, pierced right through me. I tried to sit back, but his fingers, dry as dust, increased their pressure on my wrist, their grip surprisingly strong.

"Take me," he repeated. "Day after day I look out of this window and I think of my wife's and my daughter's and my grandchildren's graves. They lie buried in the black soil of that little hill which overlooks my fields, my orchard, the forest, the brook, the mountains. Young man, don't deny an old man his last request." He looked hopeful, yet desperate. "My life has been long and painful," he continued. "Is it not unnatural when the old outlive the young? I have shared my life with you. Take me along, and I will cancel the debt."

I said nothing. Taking this old man would be a tremendous nuisance. The old codger could barely hike to the toilet . . . I tried to pull back my hands, but he refused to let them go.

161

"I can show you places and introduce you to people you would never otherwise meet. You won't regret it, I assure you," he wheezed.

The old man had me over a barrel. If I didn't take him, he wouldn't see me again and I wouldn't hear the rest of the story. All my work to date would, in that case, essentially be in vain. I had all the background information, but nothing on what took place under The General's rule; and that was what it was all about. Nor did I doubt that he could introduce me to people and show me places off the beaten track.

"Okay!" I said finally. "I'll take you. I don't know how I'll manage it, but I'll do it. I was planning to leave for Amîd on Monday."

A marvelous smile lit up his face and he let go of my wrists. "Good, very good," he said. "Buy one-way airplane tickets for Urfa instead. From Urfa we will take the bus to Amîd, and from there we will travel to Bezal."

"One way airplane tickets?" I asked suspiciously, surprised that Jesus even thought of flying.

"You won't want to travel all the way back to Urfa for your return flight. It is much shorter to fly back from Amîd." The old man had taken charge.

～～～

I told my father about taking Jesus with me. He said nothing. He merely reached into his jacket and pulled out a piece of paper with some names, and a telephone number written on it.

"Family," he said. "Memorize and destroy," he added.

I spent that evening dubbing my interviews with Jesus. The following morning I took a taxi to the other side of town, then walked the streets until I was certain no one was trailing me. I finally walked into a bank I'd never been in before, hired a safety-deposit box, and left the original cassettes there. When I got back home I hid the key in our basement storage locker.

JESUS LEADS ME

Travelling with Jesus turned out to be less difficult than I had feared. He was in fine fettle, more energetic than I had ever seen him before. He also turned out to be a first-rate tour guide. I pushed him all over Urfa's uneven, cobbled streets in a rented wheelchair while he, his head bobbling willy-nilly, showed me the sights: mosques, caves, the covered market, and his former business place. That evening we ate chicken kebab beside the fishponds.

"What happened to the business?" I shouted. I was becoming accustomed to having people twenty metres away ogle us whenever I asked a question.

Jesus looked at me across the table, and a faraway look clouded his eyes. "You remember the civil war which brought The General to power?" he began. I nodded; I'd been in grade school at the time. "There was anarchy in the land then, and the rebel leader's men extorted money from businesses," Jesus continued. "We had to pay, or they would have destroyed everything. Well, as you know, The General won the war, and he wreaked revenge on anyone he suspected of collaborating with the enemy. One night, soon after the rebel leader's arrest, the secret police broke into our house. They led us away — Meryem, Metin, Misak, little Mary and myself — and kept us for many days. They tortured us, hoping to extract information we didn't have." Jesus unbuttoned his shirt, lifted his undershirt and showed me his belly and chest. I became embarrassingly aware that we were in a public place. People turned to gape at the old man, but he was oblivious of the spectacle he was creating.

"Look," he said, "this is what they did." Long, old scars, stripes darker than the surrounding skin, covered the wrinkled, scrawny chest and sunken stomach. "The only way to tell if a tortured man is confessing the truth, spreading misinformation, or simply spouting whatever he thinks his tormentors want to hear, is through the application of more torture," Jesus added. "We were eventually released, all of us, that is, except Misak. We never saw him again."

Jesus' voice quivered, but continued speaking. "The store had been ransacked and burned, and our house raided. That week I sent Metin across the border to tell Joshua about the misfortune that had befallen us. I couldn't go myself, because I had to take care of Meryem and Mary. The police had done awful things to them both." The old man was staring over my shoulder. "It was a miracle that Metin got across. Would that he never had . . . "

The voice dropped again, and I wondered what was coming. "Border security was much tighter," Jesus said, picking up the thread of his story. To cross the minefields we would drive a couple of donkeys pulling a log ahead of us. Donkeys are cheap, you see. Metin lost both donkeys on the way over. That rarely happened before. When Joshua and Metin tried to get back with the money, they lost the first donkey before they were a quarter of the way across. The military had added more mines and changed the patterns. They were three-quarters of the way when they lost the second donkey. They decided to risk it and crawled forward. Joshua crawled onto a mine. The guards shot Metin in the barbed wire. The explosions had alerted them."

All was quiet in the open-air restaurant. The old man had just described, in the simplest of terms, the death of my father's uncle and nephews. I stared numbly in his direction. I was aware of a faint buzzing sound inside my skull. Then Jesus' lips started moving again, and I looked at them with unholy fascination, for I was incapable of looking into his eyes.

"We learned what had happened from the secret police. They came and showed me Joshua and Metin's identity cards. 'Metin was your son. Who was the man with him?' they asked. If I admitted that Joshua was my twin brother they would, of course, realize I wasn't Salih Aslan, but Jesus, son of Joseph. They would learn that we had been smuggling, and they would torture me until I confessed that we had supplied the rebels. And, in truth, Joshua had supplied the rebels, though always through other inter-mediaries.

"'Metin is my son,' I said truthfully, 'but I don't know the other man.' They threatened and bullied, and I broke down and wept. 'Please leave me to grieve my sons,' I said. Amazingly, they left, but they said they'd be back.

"I had some money and jewelry hidden in a secret place. I retrieved it and Meryem, Mary and I hired a cab. It took us to Amîd, dropping us in the middle of its busy market. We then took the first bus to Beytushebab. The next morning we started hiking to Bezal. We stopped at my parental house. The son of the old Kurd who had welcomed me years before remembered me, served us tea and loaned us a donkey, and that's how I led Meryem and Mary to Bezal.

"Abdul Kerim was still alive. He was very old by this time, even older than I am now. He welcomed us as if we were his own flesh, and we took care of him until the day he died. When he lay on his deathbed, I cabled Reward and he came in time for the funeral. I offered to buy Abdul Kerim's cottage and plot of land from him, but Reward wouldn't hear of it. He gave us the land; he had the title deeds transferred to me when he got back to the city. With the money I had rescued from Urfa I bought the orchard. Meryem, Mary and I lived on that little farm for the rest of their lives . . . They were happy years . . . " Jesus put his head in his hands and I thought he was going to cry. He managed to control himself.

〜〜〜

My purported reason for the trip to that remote and troubled part of our country was to write a series of human-interest stories. We rented a car in Urfa, which allowed us to take detours and stop when and where we wanted. We visited the neo-Hittite city of Carchemish, we photographed the nearly extinct bald ibis, and listened to the complaints of sharecroppers living in beehive houses in Harran. I left Jesus in a teahouse in Kahta while I climbed up to the silent colossi sitting silently in rows on Mount Nemrut, their two-metre-high heads, toppled off their shoulders by earthquakes, staring blindly across the valley. I interviewed engineers who enthused about the hydro-electric dams and man-made lakes they were building on the Tigris and Euphrates rivers, dams that were turning languid, dusty villages into bustling market towns, lakeside resorts or factory cities. We drove eastwards along the old Berlin to Baghdad railroad running along our southern border, and visited the ancient town of Nusaybin, now a dusty relic of its celebrated past. On the way there Jesus pointed out where they used to cross no-man's land into Syria.

I was surprised at the vast distances we had to travel, as well as continually on the lookout for lurking potholes. A shower had filled them with water, so it was impossible to judge their depth or capacity for damage. However, the area also boasted numerous other, more pleasant surprises: unmarked castles avowed the area's long, complicated, eventful history. Farmers rhythmically swung sickle and scythe through amber fields while their women threshed and winnowed in windswept places. The people, though reticent, were friendly until they saw the recording equipment. Then they would clam shut. Fear was a tangible, omnipresent reality.

When we started the drive north from Nusaybin to the old Syriac city of Hasankeyf, and then on to Mardin and Amîd, Jesus took charge once again. "Turn here," he'd say. "Follow this path to the apple orchard and turn right." I would do as he said, coercing the long-suffering rental vehicle along an overgrown track into some valley or up some hill, until we reached the remains of a village.

"Photograph the place," Jesus would order. "This is the village of Ka'lit Mara. It had three churches, Mor Shmuni, Mor Ivennis and Mor Girgis. See if you can find them." Or he would say, "This is the village of Benebil. It had four churches: Mother Mary, Mor Jakup, Mor Kuryakus and Mor Stefanos. Those ruins on the hillside are the remains of the monasteries Mor Behnam, and Mor Stefanos." Or he might say, "This is the village of Mansuriye. Until 1981 people worshipped God in those ruins there. That there used to be the Mor Barsavmo church." Or, "This is the village of Killit. There were once four monasteries here: Mor Abay, Mor Theoduto, Mor Shabay and Mor Dimet."

Although the houses might be reduced to overgrown rubble, the interlocking stone walls of the churches and monasteries defied both time and The General. I had no trouble believing Jesus' claim that their remains dated back to the fourth and fifth centuries. There were old, square bell towers, decaying doorways, domes and archways framed with time-worn Armenian or Aramaic inscriptions and ancient graveyards with reliefs of intricately worked flowers and crosses on the leeward side of weather-beaten tombstones. The size of some of the buildings was impressive; the area must once have been densely populated.

Even the untrained eye could see that much of the destruction and ruination was recent. The adobe walls of the houses and stores had tumbled but not eroded. The roofs of the churches had caved in, but their wooden beams were still in place. Though exposed to the elements, the frescoes seemed fresh and alive.

Not all the villages were deserted. Sometimes poor Kurds had moved into the ruins. They had coaxed the fields and orchards back to life and had turned the churches into mosques, or workshops, or coffeehouses. They told me that they had moved into the area two, or four, or six, or eight, or ten years earlier. Whenever I inquired about the area's previous occupants they would shrug their shoulders and walk away. They knew they were living on borrowed time, that they would share the same fate as the original inhabitants, the Christians who had lived there since time immemorial.

Although the media was under strict orders not to mention the subject, The General's systematic efforts at depopulating the South-East was the subject of numerous whispered conversations in both chic cafes and dingy tea-houses. The growing number of army body bags returning from the area didn't make the cause any more popular either, though they seemed to steel The General's resolve even more. The army would give the inhabitants forty-eight hours to get out, and then move in with bulldozers. The ostensible reason was to stamp out dissent and punish the villagers for supporting the rebels. "We will dry the swamp to catch the fish," The General had declared. There was, however, another, more substantial reason for the ruthless demographic changes, a reason we, the country's intellectuals could appreciate. It was the reason why the media had not protested overmuch at The General's actions.

The General was determined to turn our country into a powerful nation. In order to accomplish that, he had to stimulate industrialization. In order to industrialize, however, he had to increase agricultural productivity, and the way to do that was to get rid of the peasants. Although the land reforms of the sixties had driven many share-croppers off the land, much of it was still worked by peasants who walked from their villages to the small plots they continued to till in time-honoured fashion. They produced food all right, but only enough for themselves. Precious little of their produce left the villages for the big cities where the factories were, where it was needed to feed the industrial proletariat. And so The General had decreed that the agricultural process needed to be rationalized. This meant levelling the villages, and forcing the inhabitants into the cities. There they would be "integrating into the market economy", which meant they had to buy the things they needed, the things the factories produced. The plots, which had been handed down from father to son since the beginning of time, were amalgamated into large holdings and sold to entrepreneurs, who could extract the highest possible yields from the ancient soil.

Evidence of the success of The General's policy was overwhelming. Everywhere there were deserted villages surrounded by acres and acres of golden wheat nodding gently in the breeze. Sometimes we could see huge combine-harvesters reaping and threshing the grain, and pouring it into trucks that sped towards the cities as soon as they were loaded.

~~~~~

The further eastward we drove, the more frequently we hit roadblocks. The soldiers, blue-bereted commandos, were firm but polite.

"Where did you come from?"

"We flew into Urfa, and rented the car there."

"Where are you going?"

"We're making our way to Mardin. Then on to Amîd."

"What is the purpose of your visit?"

"The old man, my father's uncle, insisted on seeing the place where he grew up before he died," I'd say, then paste an inane grin on my face. "I was chosen for the mission, and here we are!" At that point the interrogating officer would smile faintly, stoop down and take a closer look at Jesus.

"Could I see your identification papers?"

"Certainly." The officer would scrutinize the hard plastic, and then glance from the photographs to our faces to see if they matched.

"You say the old man is your father's uncle? How come the names differ?"

"He is my late grandmother's brother."

At that point the eyebrows would rise. "Ah, I see... Could you open the trunk please?"

"Sure." I'd open the trunk and they'd examine the folded wheelchair and rummage through our clothes.

"Are the roads safe?" I'd ask. "No sign of rebels?"

"They keep a low profile during the day. Don't travel at night." And then they'd wave us through.

Jesus was bemused when I told him I'd described him as my father's uncle. "Your late grandmother's brother, eh?" he said. "That's a good one. I like it."

～～～

We reached Mardin at noon. Mardin is an ancient little town perched on the side of a high butte, crowned with a very old castle and immense, ultra-modern radar domes that The General uses to keep an eye on his southern enemy on behalf of his NATO allies.

The late summer heat was suffocating the place. The bright sun reflecting off the white-walled sandstone houses, stores, mosques and churches hurt the eye, and the narrow cobbled streets choked off any relieving breeze. Men and animals lounged lethargically in the scarce shade. Government officials nodded at their desks, shopkeepers dozed over their wares, the *imam* snored in the mosque courtyard and the few Syriac monks who maintained the monastery of Deyr ul Zafaran napped in their cells, their matted beards sticking to their black, sweat-drenched robes.

We pulled up to a teahouse. Sultry music and the sleepy drone of a ceiling fan wafted from the open window. I heaved Jesus into his chair and wheeled him in. Some Kurds, grouped around one of the tables, were staring at a belly dancer twisting on a television screen. Her legs, sliced from the rest of her body by a wavering line, seemed to dance apart from her torso. The other customers, clustered in threes and fours, sipped tea and lazily pushed backgammon stones. A young boy moved among the tables delivering beverages and collecting empty glasses.

"Two cold Colas!"

The boy reached into a cooler, opened the bottles and set them before us.

"Tea!"

The boy filled up the village Kurds' glasses.

"Coffee!" A Syrian cattle dealer waved his arm to draw the boy's attention.

The belly dancer reached her crescendo. The Kurds, eyes glistening, were glued to the set. The crackling music picked up speed, the dancer whirled, thrust out her hips and flung her legs in a final flurry.

"The End." The words were divided by the same line that had bisected the dancer. The Kurds came out of their trance and shuffled to their feet. One of them paid the bill, extracting the money from a leather pouch attached to his belt with a chain. They tramped into the blinding heat, banging the door behind them. The fan droned, a fly flew in large, lazy circles.

Ding, dong, ding, dong. A church bell began pealing pure and clear through the stultifying air. Ding, dong, ding, dong. It was a pleasant sound, such as I had never heard before. Mardin was one of the few areas in my country where sufficient Christians remained to warrant a church bell.

The bell ringer seemed to be pulling furiously at the ropes, and the sound swelled as it reverberated through the streets, the alleys, the teahouse, echoing off the mosque walls and filling the courtyards.

Ding, dong, ding dong.

The hoarse, electric crackling of an amplifier, followed by a cough and a grunt, interrupted the bells. The call to prayer followed:

"God is great! God is great!"

Ding dong, ding dong.

"God is . . . "

Ding

"Great"

Dong.

The *imam* did his duty perfunctorily, but the bells kept ringing.

Ding, dong, ding, dong.

"What's going on? Why does that crazy Jakup keep ringing the bells?" someone asked.

A swarthy man with a huge mustache walked through the door. "Bad news," he said to everyone present. "Pretty Gazela has passed away." His words roused the teahouse from its somnolent state, and conversations started simultaneously at the tables around us, conversations carried out in serious tones and accompanied by the shaking of heads and the clucking of tongues.

"May God forgive her sins and accept her soul."

"At least she's not suffering any more."

"She was young. Too young."

"A bad omen. God's got things mixed up again. A grand-father lives, and a young bride dies."

"Death strikes when and where it wills."

Ding, dong. Ding, dong.

"Poor thing."

"God accept her soul."

Ding . . .

"Pretty Gazela . . . "

"Mercy, but it wasn't her turn . . . "

. . . dong.

"The old live, and the young are taken. It's a bad omen."

Ding . . .

"Remember her carefree walk?"

"Remember how she would dance at weddings and circumcisions?"

. . . dong.

"Who'll look after her children?"

"Old Aziz, I suppose."

"Its not fair . . . the old live and the young die . . . God's got things mixed up again . . . "

Ding, dong . . .

Jesus tugged at my sleeve. "Let's leave," he said. There was a haunting look in his eyes. I paid the bill and pushed him back to the car. He managed to get out of the chair and into the front seat by himself. We left town and headed for Amîd.

"The old live and the young die . . . A bad omen . . . God's got things mixed up again," he muttered.

Ding, dong.

I wondered how he'd managed to hear what was said.

Ding . . . dong . . . The last peal travelled mournfully down the hill and over the wheat fields and gullies until it reached the stream, where its last vibrations mixed with the gentle murmur of the river.

Family Reunion

Jesus' descriptions of Amîd, or Black Amîd, as the Kurds also call it, were accurate, though dated. The city had grown far beyond its ancient black basalt walls. Concrete buildings and asphalt roads with open gutters running on either side now covered the tomato fields into which Jesus' donkey had bolted. The watermelons were, indeed, everything he claimed them to be. The huge forty and fifty kilogram monsters were grown in pits dug in the fertile soil along the riverbanks, with pigeon droppings used as fertilizer. As we approached the city we could see donkeys hauling the immense fruits up the hill one or two at a time.

Jesus flushed with pleasure when we pulled up to the old Tigris hotel. It wasn't exactly as posh as he had made it out to be, but then he had described it as it had been during the Second World War, and through the eyes of a villager seeing luxury for the first time. Even if the place was worse for wear, it had preserved something of its Victorian-era glory. The carpets, though threadbare and faded, were still red, and the lobby was lined with clouded and cracked mirrors. Jesus bobbed his head excitedly in the direction of the bellhop and winked conspiratorially, as if the faded fez on the man's head was irrefutable evidence establishing the veracity of everything he had told me in the course of numerous interviews. I had to laugh at his delightful naiveté and his childlike delight at being back in Amîd. Taking Jesus had been a good move.

Once we were settled in our room, I dialed the number my father had told me to memorize. A deep voice, speaking the dense accent of the region, picked up the other end of the line.

"Hello?"

"Good evening. Could I speak to Mr. Kemal please?"

"Who are you?" The voice was suspicious.

"I am Tarik Kemal, the son of Selim Kemal." There was a moment's silence; I could hear the man breathing as he processed this information.

"What do you want?" he said finally.

"I was hoping to get to know my uncles and cousins. Mr. Kemal is my father's brother, and his sons are my cousins."

There was another period of silence before the man responded. "Where are you phoning from?"

"From here in Amîd. The Tigris hotel."

"Are you alone?"

"No, I'm travelling with an old man, a friend who used to live here."

"How long are you here for?"

"Well, I was just hoping to meet some family. We're not planning to stay long. I promised the old man we'd visit his childhood village, and then it's back home." I tried to sound carefree, but the man's suspicious nature disturbed me. I had looked forward to getting acquainted with real family, but the man's hesitancy put a damper on my anticipation.

"Okay," the voice said. "We'll come to the hotel after evening prayers tomorrow."

"Great!" I said, trying to sound enthusiastic. "We'll meet you down in the lobby." There was no reply.

The following day I pushed Jesus all over town. We went through the Hanchepek district of the Infidel Quarter, but the infidels were all gone; the area was overrun with displaced Kurds instead. Nor were there any Jews left in the Jewish quarter. An old Kurd there told us that they had all pulled up stakes and left for Israel on the same day, many years ago. There was no sign of Syriacs in their traditional quarter between the Urfa and Mardin gates either, excepting the few old women lighting candles and mumbling incomprehensible prayers in front of some faded icons in the church of the Virgin Mary. The Chaldean church had been turned into a mosque.

We took off our shoes and went into the building. An air of sadness hung about Jesus as he looked around the place of worship.

"It is all over," he said, "The church has become a mosque. Why should it be otherwise? Did not even I, Jesus, son of Joseph, the last of my people, live my life as the Muslim Salih, son of Abdul Kerim?"

I wheeled him away from there and pushed him to the teahouse of Mahmut the Kurd. The place was under new ownership and freshly decorated, but in Jesus' mind it was still the teahouse of Mahmut the Kurd where he had eked out a living, where he and Joshua had met. Once again, he was quiet and withdrawn, lost in his own memories.

Eventually he started speaking. His voice was low, like someone confessing a crippling sin or a heinous crime.

"During the first part of my life I was true to myself. I lived a lie then, too, but it was a lie I longed to shed the moment I discovered the truth," he said. "But when I discovered the truth, I didn't discard the lie. I reverted back to it. Jesus, son of Joseph, embraced Salih, son of the Muslim Abdul Kerim, so tightly that he smothered the truth. The first life of Salih, son of Abdul Kerim, was a disguise given me by the grace of God, a disguise I wore lightly until He in His mercy saw fit to reveal the reality beneath. But when I discovered the reality I clung to the disguise, hoping it would stand me in better stead. But God will not be mocked. I am culpable for the second life of Salih, son of Abdul Kerim, and God responded by taking away the last vestiges of the reality . . . " Tears flowed from his eyes. "When I finally discarded the disguise, it was too late," he whispered. "It was too late . . . too late . . . " He kept repeating the words. "Too late . . . too late . . . " His head hung down and tears stained his shirt.

~~~

It was early afternoon when we got back to the hotel. I wheeled him to our room, undressed him and tucked him into bed. He slept, tossing and turning restlessly, until I woke him up during the evening call to prayer. We showered, put on clean clothes and went down to the lobby to wait.

We waited for nearly an hour. Just as I began to wonder if the suspicious Uncle Kemal would show up at all, the front door opened and a man with my father's eyes and forehead entered. Two men about my own age accompanied him. I stood up, and my Uncle Kemal approached me and shook my hand.

"You must be Tarik," he said. "Welcome to Amîd. I am Ahmet Kemal."

My uncle was a polite, well-dressed man who, like my father, carried himself with a certain reserve. I took his hand, kissed it and lifted it to my forehead.

"Peace be with you," I said. "It is good to meet family." I shook hands with the two young men who introduced themselves as Zekai and Musa. They were my uncle's sons, my cousins. Both had well-manicured, longish beards and were dressed in dark jackets and baggy trousers. One of them wore a shirt with the upright white collar favoured by Muslim clerics, the other fingered his worry beads incessantly.

"Forgive me for not coming last night," my uncle said. I sensed he was genuinely embarrassed. "This is Kurdistan," he added with a rueful smile.

I understood. While we were visiting the Infidel Quarter, the Chaldean church and Mahmut the Kurd's teahouse, he had run a check on us. I was sure now that we had been followed.

"This is Kurdistan." A simple sentence pregnant with meaning. Kurdistan, where every rebel advance is cheered and The General's brutal hand omnipresent. Kurdistan, where barbed wire and roadblocks are everywhere, where nervous conscripts brandish automatic rifles on street corners, where rumbling tanks, their turrets waving menacingly from left to right, dominate the streets, and where sluggish helicopters and screaming jets whine overhead. Kurdistan, where the police infiltrate every tribe, every clan and every household, teaching people to be wary and distrustful of everyone at all times.

My uncle invited us into his car. Jesus got into the front seat while I sat in the back with my two cousins. Everyone was quiet for the duration of the journey; impenetrably so, I thought, as though they feared that their own vehicle might be bugged. We drove through a bewildering tangle of narrow roads and alleys until we came to a heavy wooden doorway built into a rubble wall. A small roof sheltered the entryway from the sun and rain. We got out of the car and stepped through the doorway into one of Amîd's grand, traditional houses. We followed my uncle across the courtyard, where a fountain played gently, to a scrupulously clean, vaulted room. There he bid us to sit down. We removed our shoes and sat on mattresses on the floor. One of my cousins helped Jesus out of his wheelchair, and placed him in the place of honour, in the middle of the mattress away from the doorway. Jesus sat down with a satisfied grunt.

A girl, covered from head to toe in a black *chador*, spread a large plastic sheet on the floor, and we gathered cross-legged around it. The girl scattered dishes with different types of nuts, along with several bowls of rock sugar, onto the plastic sheet, and then she poured tea into little glasses. My uncle handed the glasses around, beginning with Jesus. The men reached for the sugar bowl, placed a lump of rock sugar between their teeth and sipped their tea through it. I imitated them like an expert.

My uncle and cousins largely ignored Jesus; he was old and frail, deaf and insignificant, no threat to anyone. It was obvious, however, that they were sizing me up. They asked me about my father's health, and about my mother and sisters. When they learned that my parents were divorced, their disapproval lay heavy in the air, and when they discovered that I worked for *The Morning* I sensed their reproof afresh. The left-of-centre newspaper's regular lambasting of Islamic extremism made it one of the fundamentalists' favourite hate targets.

The beards, the collars, the worry beads, the *chador* all indicated that my family took religion seriously. Nevertheless, they were scrupulously polite. Musa said little, but Zekai mentioned that he had seen my name in print, but that it hadn't occurred to him that the writer might be a relative. Some other men drifted into the courtyard and joined us around the plastic sheet. They greeted each other politely, going around the circle shaking hands and kissing each other on both cheeks. I was introduced as their half-cousin from Istanbul. They nodded politely and the conversation turned, inevitably, to that most sensitive and inimical triad of subjects: religion, The General, the rebel movement.

Other than watching them vent their spleens on the square on Friday afternoons, I had had little contact with the fundamentalists. The motivation behind the rebel campaign — The General's policy of ethnic cleansing in Kurdistan — I could understand. I had little sympathy for the fundamentalists' conspiracy theories and hopes of turning the clock back to the Middle Ages.

The men around me spoke with repressed agitation. Their conversations drifted from new anti-Islamic legislation to the possibility that the CIA was sponsoring the explosion of western-style discos across the country, and from the closure of a local Koranic school to the influx of Western professionals whom The General had invited to help him modernize the economy. Several discussions swirled around me. I tried to make sense of the snatches of disjointed sentences uttered with suppressed, fanatical animation:

" . . . turned the country into a Western dependency . . . "

" . . . the Jews are manipulating him. He's under their thumb . . . "

" . . . a Freemason . . . "

" . . . new world order . . . American dominance . . . "

" . . . the Jews control the purse strings . . . "

No matter how involved he was in conversation, my uncle kept a close eye on the tea glasses. Whenever one was empty, he would signal the girl in black and she would refill it instantly. When a guest had had enough to drink he'd lay his glass on its side.

" . . . American and British oil interests . . . "

" . . . Armenian terrorism supported by Russian imperialists . . . "

" . . . possibility of a jihad against NATO bases and Western interests . . . "

" . . . Christian conspiracy . . . "

" . . . the Illuminate in conjuction with the Vatican . . . "

" . . . his mother was a Christian, his father an Alawite . . . "

They tried to draw me into the conversation, but I responded with non-committal grunts until I was sidelined. I was content to observe and listen to the amazing nonsense so sincerely believed, and began to appreciate why my father found that he had little in common with his family.

The black-clad girl reappeared with a large, round tray piled high with rice, pine nuts, aubergine, and pieces of chicken. A second girl, also in black, entered with a pile of plates, which my uncle proceeded to fill to overflowing.

I wondered whether the girls were also cousins, but was afraid to ask.

The men muttered "In the name of God, the merciful, the compassionate", lifted their spoons and turned toward their plates. The conversation fell silent; only quiet crunching sounds and the odd belch disturbed the silence. Eating was serious business.

Suddenly there was a stir. One of the daughters appeared in the doorway, gesticulating nervously. My uncle jumped up and left the room, to reappear a moment later, ushering in an old man. He was very stooped, had a thin, neatly trimmed white beard. He must have had Parkinsons disease, for his head and hands shook visibly. When he appeared my cousins and most of the other guests jumped up from their places, grasped the old man's hand, kissed it and touched it to their foreheads and said in Kurdish,

"Tu bi xair hati, agha me" "Welcome, our agha!"

I stood up to show my respect and went to kiss his hand. The old man leaned heavily on my uncle's arm as he held out his hand for me.

"Welcome," he said. His voice was raspy, as it often is with old people, but pleasant. "Are they feeding you enough?" He had a kindly smile and his mind appeared keen.

"Plenty," I affirmed, and he nodded approvingly. "Good, good."

The man was ancient, even more so than the Jesus, I suspected. Jesus had lived a rough life. This old patriarch, on the other hand, was rich. I noticed a Rolex on his wrist, and the cloth in his traditional baggy trousers and shirt were of the best quality. His hadji's skullcap was made of fine linen.

My uncle led the old agha to the head of the mattress. I moved my plate to clear a space, and the old man sat beside Jesus in the place of honour.

Jesus, who'd been in a bit of a reverie to that point, looked at the newcomer beside him with a peculiar fascination. The old man, evidently becoming aware of Jesus' stare, turned to him, smiled mildly, and held out his hand. Jesus took it.

"Welcome, guest of God," the old man said. Jesus smiled, nodded politely, and then pointed to his ear to indicate he was deaf. The old agha sighed sympathetically, bobbed his head understandingly, and turned toward the food. My uncle filled up his plate; the agha picked up his spoon and, with a shaking hand, lifted it to his mouth, dropping half the contents on the way.

"Father, can I pour you some tea?" my uncle asked.

"I'll have it afterwards", he rasped gently. He was concentrating with furled brow on transporting another spoonful of pilav to his mouth without spilling the contents on the way. When he succeeded he grunted with satisfaction.

"Shall I help you, Father?" my uncle asked.

"No, no, I can help myself, as you can see," he said smiling pleasantly, and dug the spoon into the plate. I grinned to myself: the man had too much self-respect to have others feeding him before guests.

My uncle reached across me to place a piece of cloth on the old man's lap. "Here, Father, a napkin," he said.

I was slow on the uptake that evening, but at that point something began to register; I found myself turning involuntarily to stare at the kindly, bumbling old man beside me. Three times my uncle had addressed this old man as "father". If that is so, he must be my grandfather, I slowly grasped. The thought took my breath away. I had never considered that my grandfather, my father's father might still be alive!

When I was a child my father had suggested he was dead, yet here he was: the coward, the Armenian Butcher, the soldier with the golden epaulets Jesus had described in his first interview with me. Here was the man who had raped my grandmother, taken away her child, my father, and dumped her on the streets of a strange city! I could feel my skin begin to crawl as I looked at the guileless creature fumbling beside me.

The agha must have become aware of Jesus' intense gaze, for he turned toward him a second time.

"Excuse me, but I don't think they told me who you are?" he asked kindly, yet as loud as his old voice box permitted.

I will never know how Jesus understood the question. Maybe he lip-read it, or maybe he'd sensed its meaning intuitively.

"I am this boy's father's uncle," Jesus answered with a conspiratorial wink in my direction. "I am the brother of his late grandmother . . . "

Time then gradually slowed down and ground to a halt, until the silence of eternity hung precariously in the air. I saw my uncle's mind clicking into gear and my cousin's brows furling.

"Who did you say you were?" the old man between us demanded again, breaking that momentary spell of infinity. He leaned toward Jesus, his eyes squinting intensely. "I don't think I understood," he added.

My uncle lifted his arms and half rose as if in defense, then fell down in defeat as Jesus put his lips to the man's ear and shouted as loud as his feeble chest let him.

"My name is Jesus, son of Joseph. I am this boy's father's uncle. I am the brother of his late grandmother!".

I do not believe that, at the time, Jesus knew he was telling the truth. He was smiling broadly as he spoke and, as far as he was concerned, was merely keeping up the charade we had used at the roadblocks. But the truth it was, and it hit like a bomb with a delayed fuse. When Jesus' words penetrated the old man's brain he turned to face his former wife's brother.

"You are Hanbak's brother?" he shouted vehemently. "From what hell did you arise to eat food in my house! God curse the both of you! Who let you in?!" The old man's chest rose and fell dangerously as he spat the words into Jesus' face and the veins across his temple turned purple and throbbed. I have witnessed numerous ugly incidents in my journalistic career, but have never seen such a rapid transformation from the benign to the sadistic. I had come looking for flesh and blood, and recoiled from what I found.

Jesus reacted confusedly at the sudden deluge of hatred. "Wh . . . What do you mean?" He stammered. "Who are you . . . Hanbak . . . ? They took her away . . . Joshua said . . . they took her away in the night . . . Do you know where they took her . . . ?" Jesus started breathing in short, staccato bursts; I feared he might hyperventilate.

My grandfather turned and shouted at my uncle. "Did you let these infidels in? Throw them out! I want them out! They'll pollute you with their lies like they polluted your half-brother, the socialist lackey! God curse them all! Out!"

The man's face grew even more livid, blue veins on his forehead started protruding menacingly, and foam sprayed from his mouth. Neither before nor since have I witnessed such wanton, baseless, ugly hatred. The old man was breathing heavily but kept on ranting. I got to my feet and stepped rudely over the rabid creature, and held Jesus protectively.

"Tarik," Jesus asked plaintively. "What's going on?" His eyes searched my face. "Do these people know what happened to Hanbak? Is she still alive?"

"There's nothing going on, Jesus. There's been a mistake. We're leaving," I shouted. "Get the wheelchair," I ordered my uncle. He protested feebly, but got to his feet quickly and fetched the wheelchair. No one else stirred. My uncle stood to one side while I helped Jesus into the chair. I could sense numerous murderous eyes boring into me. My grandfather kept up his hateful haranguing, while my uncle followed me as I pushed Jesus out of the room.

"You shouldn't have done this," he said quietly. "Your old man set you up to this, didn't he?"

That's when I turned on him. "Now I understand why Father won't have anything to do with you," I spat out. "Your self-righteousness, your irrational hates, your idiotic religious notions and your ridiculous conspiracy theories have so twisted, so distorted reality that you can't even accept your own flesh and blood!" I looked across at the old man. "I know all about you," I shouted hatefully from the threshold. "You're the coward of the Arab front, the Armenian butcher, the one who dumped his wife and took her child away. Praise God, the child, my father, looked after his mother, took care of her until the day she died!"

"Out! Get out or I'll have you killed. Get rid of them!" The old man's chest heaved. My cousins jumped to their feet and pushed and jostled us into the courtyard and through the front door. It slammed shut behind us but that didn't prevent me from hearing a cacophony of recriminations erupting.

It was dark in the alley. My heart was pounding, adrenaline was making my limbs shake uncontrollably. I started pushing Jesus ahead of me up one alley and down another in the direction of the thoroughfare. He was quiet; I could see the black outline of his head bobbing up and down as I pushed the chair over the rough paving stones. I walked until we got to a café, pushed through the door and collapsed into a chair. I ordered Nescafe and cake for both of us. When it came, my hands shook so badly that I couldn't keep the coffee from spilling. Jesus didn't touch his cake and coffee. He sat in silence, clutching the sides of his wheelchair. Eventually he lifted his head and looked at me questioningly.

"Tarik, what happened? Who were those people?" His voice was low, almost imperceptible and his look was full of wretchedness, full of suffering and accusation.

"Forget what happened, Jesus," I shouted. "Those people are not whom I thought they were. I made a mistake. We shouldn't have gone there."

Jesus seemed to have shrunk and the light gone out of his eyes. He looked exceedingly old and frail, brittle almost, with the translucent quality of old crystal. It was everything I could do not to tell him the truth, and to beg him to forgive my deceit.

"Tarik, they mentioned Hanbak," he whispered. "Do they know Hanbak? Do they know what happened to her?"

"No, Jesus, they don't. Like I said, there was a mistake," I said roughly, and I loathed myself for lying. We sat quietly for some time, and then Jesus lifted his face and looked me in the eye.

"Tarik, you, too, mentioned Hanbak once . . . " My hand jerked when he said that, and coffee spilled onto my lap. I winced as the hot liquid penetrated my trouser leg.

"You must have misunderstood me. Before tonight I'd never even heard the name Hanbak before," I lied again. "It's a foreign word, isn't it? Here, let me help you eat your cake."

I lifted the fork from the table and proceeded to feed him like a baby. He didn't object.

"Tarik, promise me that you'll take me to Bezal. Take me to Meryem and Mary's graves."

"Okay." I nodded my head.

"Are you telling the truth, my boy?" His voice was barely audible.

"I promise, Jesus, I promise!" I cried. "We'll go first thing in the morning if you like."

JESUS DIES

A wounded animal recognizes instinctively when further resistance is meaningless. With its last energy it slips to a familiar corner to surrender the will to live. It then sinks into a dreamy, inert stupor, and lets the cold lassitude of death extinguish the spark of life. That, I thought afterwards, is what happened to Jesus.

He had tossed and turned restlessly in his sleep that night. I heard him cry "Hanbak", and "Joshua", and "Meryem" at various times. It was still dark when he woke up. He didn't want breakfast. He urged me to leave immediately.

We drove eastwards, straight into the mountains, straight into the vast, orange-red globe of the sun breaking over the shining pink and purple summits. The lower reaches of the sky looked as if they had been dipped in gold. Cumulus clouds piling one on top of the other filled the sky. There was no other traffic, and I could drive fast.

Jesus sat torpid and pathetic in the seat next to mine; I sensed that his spirit was broken. He was normally full of chat, commenting on the scenery, or telling stories about people he'd met, and adventures he'd had in the places we passed through. Now, however, he seemed shriveled and empty. I tried to engage him in conversation.

"Jesus, when did you leave Bezal for the city?" I shouted.

Jesus didn't reply, and I was about to repeat the question when he finally responded. "Six years ago," he said quietly.

"Why?" I asked.

"The army gave us forty-eight hours to move."

"Why did you go all the way to Istanbul? Had you been there before? Did you know anyone there?"

"We hoped to find Reward. But he had disappeared. Died, most probably. In any case, the people who lived at the address he'd given me had never heard of him." There was a flaccidity in Jesus' voice which disturbed me.

"What happened then?"

"Only Shimone and I were left. We sat in front of the Chaldean church and begged," he said listlessly. I thought of my grandmother, Jesus' sister, begging in front of the Chaldean church in Mardin, and, once again, it was everything I could do not to tell Jesus the truth. Yet I couldn't do so, I wouldn't do so, because I had to think of the future, my future; infidels have no future in The General's scheme of things. We drove in silence for some time, and then he spoke again, spoke of his own volition.

"As a beggar I finally ceased being Salih Aslan, son of the Muslim Abdul Kerim, and reclaimed my true identity as Jesus, son of Joseph. But it was too late . . . God's judgments are righteous and just . . . I had lived the lie for too long." He fell silent again, and I wondered if that was all he would say. Eventually, however, he resumed his story. Afterwards it struck me that it was as if relating his life-story to me was his last remaining duty, a duty he determined to complete successfully.

"There were still a few Chaldeans in Istanbul when we first arrived," he continued. "They were all in the process of immigrating to the west, but Shimone and I weren't eligible. There was no one to sponsor us, and, in any case, my ID card stated that I was the Muslim Salih Aslan. But some people in the church believed that I really was Jesus, son of Joseph, when I said the Lord's Prayer in Aramaic. A youngster named Melki, a good boy, found us the room on the hill. He also helped me fill in some papers, and after that we started getting a little bit of money, just enough to pay for the room. What we earned from begging was enough to feed us.

"Later, I became too old to beg; I couldn't climb the hill anymore. Shimone went out alone . . . " His voice trailed off listlessly. I thought of Shimone. Shimone serving tea and cookies. Shimone listening silently, passively, sitting poised and withdrawn on the hard-backed chair. Shimone hoisting Jesus' body when it slumped too far to one side, Shimone dismissing me with a gesture or a look. Shimone going out alone, returning with a few eggs . . .

Jesus seemed to withdraw deeper and deeper into himself in the course of that day, but he roused himself several times to tell me to leave the main road. I would obey, coaxing the hard-pressed vehicle in a wide arch over rutted fields and goat trails. He knew instinctively where the roadblocks were; we managed to dodge each one.

I asked him about Shimone. She was his granddaughter, he said, Mary's daughter. Mary had married a Kurd, a grandson of the man who had occupied his parental house in the next village. The soldiers shot him six years ago to encourage them all to move out quickly.

So, at long last, I knew the truth about Shimone. She was family, too, my second cousin. Now I knew the truth, and the knowledge added another layer to the oppressive feeling of guilt.

It was late afternoon when we arrived in Beytushebab. The sun had disappeared behind brooding clouds, the light had faded from the thick sky, and the air was warm, dark, close, full of the thick smell of the menacing cloud-mass. A somber stillness hung heavily over the town.

I was about to park in front of the inn when Jesus pointed to a hardware store down the road. "Go there," he whispered.

When we got there I looked at him questioningly. His head hung down and I had to strain my ears to be able to hear what he said. "Buy a hammer and three or four nails, two pieces of wood, a small pot of black paint, a paint-brush, and a shovel," he murmured. I did as I was told, throwing the stuff into the car's trunk. I asked no questions.

I tried to get Jesus to eat that night, but he refused all nourishment, except for a bottle of Coke. I left him in the room while I went to buy some food for myself. When I got back, he was asleep, curled in the fetal position. I, too, was tired, and fell into a deep sleep.

Jesus, fully dressed, woke me up early the next morning. He was shivering and feverish, but seemed more cheerful than the previous day. He again refused to eat, urging me to get dressed quickly instead. It was still dark when we left the inn, but then it never really got light that day. The oppressive cumulus clouds had coalesced into a thick, dark blanket that blotted out the sun.

It had been six years since the army had cleared the villages, but the land was still wasted. We reached a razed hamlet, and Jesus made me stop the car in front of a pile of debris. He looked at the ruins and tears flowed uncontrollably from his enlarged eyes; I knew that that ruin had once been the house of Joseph, Jesus' father.

I pressed hard on the accelerator and pushed the car over the pass, and into the valley on the other side. A claw of lightening cut across the sky, and in the flash of intense light the bushes and plants and trees seemed magnified, and the mountain peaks very near. It was followed by a long, deep roll of thunder. The tension in the heavy cloud-mass pressed heavily on the land.

The car tossed and swayed as it rolled down the other side of the pass, then bumped and rattled its way up the opposite hillside. I clung tightly to the steering wheel, lest it slip out of my hands and we plunge into the river below.

We crossed a field and came to a run-down orchard. Beyond the unkempt peach and plum trees lay the tumbled ruins of yet another ancient village. Its houses were reduced to rubble but the mosque, its lonely minaret etched forlornly against the dark green wall of the hills behind it, appeared intact. Jesus pointed to a path, and I swung the car onto it.

We pulled up to the ruin that I knew had been Mother Ayshe and Abdul Kerim's house. Its location perfectly matched the description Jesus had so lovingly painted: the orchard on one side, the village above it, the hills beyond, the river below. Another jagged zigzag of lightning flashing across the sky caused the ruin to leap forward; large, hot raindrops started dropping earthward, falling slowly, steadily from the overloaded sky.

Jesus got out of the vehicle. I followed him. He tottered unsteadily toward the house, and looked at it. I went back to the car, got a coat and draped it over his shoulders.

"Give me your arm, my son," he said, "and help an old man, your father's uncle, to the top of that little hill."

My heart faltered. He had arrived at the truth and I didn't know how to respond. The rain started falling steadily, the big drops atomizing into a myriad of minute splashes as they hit the hard-baked earth. I stood condemned before him.

"Come, come," he said. "There is no need to apologize. You spoke the truth at the roadblocks, and may God bless you for it. No, no, don't be afraid. I will not give your secret away. There will be no need." He clung to my arm and started shuffling up the hillock.

"Look," he said when we got to the top. "Do you see those mounds? The one on the left is Mother Ayshe. Next to her lies Abdul Kerim, then Meryem and my little girl Mary. That one there is Hasan, Mary's husband. Those two over there are grandfather and grandmother's."

I flinched when I saw the dark, overgrown mounds. Two of them, Meryem and Mary's, had a line of stones running down the middle and a second vertical row near the top, just like the cross I had formed upon grandmother's grave.

"Tell me about your grandmother," Jesus said as though he had read my mind. "Tell me about my sister Hanbak."

"She . . . ," I stammered, not knowing what to say. "She lived with us. My father took good care of her . . . She . . . had her own room . . . I used to visit her there . . . "

"Did she remain true?"

"Yes!" I screamed the affirmation. "She clung to her faith, her identity, and she even tried to form us into her image. She grasped her book so tightly we buried it with her!" My tension and guilt found expression, and the driving rain streaming down my face mixed with the salty tears and blurred my vision. "She lies in a Muslim graveyard but under a cross just like these," I sobbed and I was aware that, for the first time since my parents' divorce, I was weeping.

"Dearest Hanbak. You are better than your brothers. You were the best among us," he whispered. He looked up at me and I could read the desolation in his rheumy eyes.

"Look after Shimone," he said. "Remember, she too is family." I nodded dumbly and he spoke again. "Go back to the car now and leave me with my dead ones."

It began to pour and I protested, but he insisted that I go. "Leave me to pray," he said, so I returned to the car. I turned on the windshield wipers. Streams of water blurred Jesus' silhouette. He was kneeling in the teeming rain before the little mounds, rocking back and forth. Suddenly, a flash of lightning forked down and struck the top of the hillock, followed by a terrific tearing noise as though, close above, divinity was ripping the curtain to the Most Holy Place in two. The heavens opened and the waters cascaded as in the days of the prophet Noah. I looked to see if anything had happened to Jesus, but couldn't locate him. He was gone! I leaped out of the car and staggered up the hill, slipping on the slick soil, trying to peer through the curtain of rain. I looked everywhere, stumbling this way and that, but I couldn't find him. An eerie darkness closed in and the rain smeared my glasses. I couldn't see more than a few feet in any direction. I stumbled back to the car, turned on the engine and lit the headlights, hoping they would guide Jesus back to me.

The storm raged briefly but maniacally. The blackened trees whiplashed back and forth as though possessed, the rain beat madly, and the wind buffeted the vehicle, rocking it from left to right, as though it were some primordial giant's plaything. Then the tempest subsided. The winds dropped, the pressure lifted, and the violent downpour lessened to a steady, rhythmical cadence.

I stepped out of the car and looked around. The air was close and warm, and smelled of freshly cut grass. The trees rustled and swayed gently in the cool breeze. I pulled my collar up against the rain, and clambered up the slippery slope.

Jesus lay between the stone crosses, face up, eyes closed, his hands folded across his chest, his sodden clothes pressing his frail body into the soil. His broken glasses lay beside him, half buried in the mud. His hair was matted and dirty, but a smile illuminated his soiled countenance.

I knelt beside him, my knees sinking into the cold, waterlogged muck. My chest was a painful vacuum, and I understood that I had come to love Jesus the Infidel, my father's uncle, the last of an ethnically cleansed people, an eccentric old man torn between the call to remain faithful to his now extinct people, and the passions common to mankind.

I looked at his pale face and stroked the lifeless cheek. He had done what he could, I thought, to make his burial as easy as possible. I got up, fetched the shovel from the back of the car and dug the hole. It was not easy to dig through the sticky, rocky gumbo, but I worked steadily, like an automaton. Sweat dripped from the inside of my saturated clothes. I felt hot yet clammy, my hands were cramped and my stomach was nauseous. When the hole was dug, I took off my sopping coat and wrapped it around Jesus' head; I couldn't bring myself to throw dirt and stones into the mouth, nostrils and eyes of the man who had given me the capacity to weep, to feel, and the ability to love. I rolled the stiffening corpse into the hole and filled it as quickly as I could. I then hauled the planks and the nails up from the car, nailed a rough cross together, painted the epitaph and planted it upright at the head of the grave.

Yusuf oğlu İsa
Düşmanlarım zafer kahkahası atmasın

That is Turkish for "Jesus, son of Joseph. Let not my enemies triumph over me." I wished I knew the Aramaic.

The wind died and it ceased to rain. There was no sound other than the barely audible dripping of water from shrubs and trees, the trickling of numerous rivulets flowing downhill, and the faint shriek of a bird fussing on the embankment of the river below.

Epilogue

That, then, is the story of Jesus the Infidel. As for me, I was arrested when I got back to Amîd. Eventually they charged me with illegal internment of a body. It took my father nearly three months to grease the right palms to secure my release.

While I was incarcerated, the secret police raided our house. Father said they behaved very politely. The officer in charge, a philatelist, was extremely taken with my stamp collection. He offered to buy the doubles, but Father told him he didn't think I wanted to part with them. They left, taking the notes and cassettes I had set aside for them. I eventually recovered the originals from the safety deposit box; they form the basis of this book.

Soon after I returned home I took a taxi to the hill. I got off in the red light district and climbed up to the wooden house in the slum above the harbour, the one with a humble little room at the top of a rickety staircase and with red geraniums in the window. In response to my knock, a haggard looking woman hung her head out of the casement.

"Yes?"

"I'm looking for someone named Shimone." I noticed that the geraniums were gone.

"No one here by that name."

"Did the previous occupant leave a forwarding address?"

"No."

"You have any idea where she went?"

"Never met the previous occupants. We moved in ten days ago."

I wandered slowly down the hill, stopping to greet Hampar and Misto, Andreas Stephanopolis and Shukru, Mahmut and Aziz. I told them that Jesus had died, and their grief was genuine, as was their fear; they were next in line. I asked them about Shimone and they said they didn't know what had become of her, yet I sensed that they were holding something back.

I hadn't meant to, but when I reached the red-light district my feet moved of their own volition to the window in which the beautiful girl I once hated used to sit. I wanted to see her one last time. I peered through the window, but there was no one there. There were no books lying around, either. I squatted beside the garbage bin on the other side of the street and waited. Eventually a fat, swarthy man stepped out of the doorway and got into a taxi. Soon afterwards the curtain behind the window fluttered and a beautiful girl, with long black hair that fell to the small of her back, appeared behind the glass. I ran across the street and pressed my face against the glass. Shimone looked at me, and a look of hatred spread across her face. Then she started rolling her tongue over her lips, though her eyes remained full of detestation, filled with loathing. We stared at each other, then I turned my back on her and flagged down a cab. I thought of Shimone serving me tea and fruit; Shimone sacrificing herself for an ignorant old man. Love can be powerful, I thought.

My heart was in turmoil and, briefly, I hated Jesus for compelling me to make a vow I wouldn't keep. Yet he had done that which was right; his last concern was for another. How different Jesus had been from my father and me, I thought. We were wealthy and had connections, yet were incapable of risking anything for the sake of someone else, even if they were family. We were no better than the fundamentalists who had rejected us, and worse than Shimone, who'd sold herself for Jesus. I loathed myself for it, but knew that neither my father nor I had the wherewithal for sacrificial love. We deserved the lonely, meaningless existence we so tightly embraced.

Author's Postscript

The story of Jesus the Infidel is so true, that even I am unable to determine where fiction takes over from fact.

Those familiar with Turkish Kurdistan will recognize the cities and the landscape. Amîd, Urfa, Mardin, Bezal, the Zagros, and every other place mentioned is — or was — as described. Because I opted for the Kurdish place names instead of the officially sanctioned ones, the reader will not find the words "Amîd" or "Bezal" in his atlas. Amîd is called Diyarbakir by non-Kurds; Bezal ceased to exist in the 1990s. Its fate is recounted accurately.

When I first trekked through Turkish Kurdistan in 1983, I could still visit a number of Chaldean villages. Today there are none. In all of Turkey, in fact, only a mere thirty or thirty-five Chaldean families remain, living in areas of Istanbul called Dolapdere, Kasimpaşa and Karaköy. "The Hill" is a collage of these areas as they were during the 1980s.

"The Square" is described much as it was when I was a student at the University of Istanbul. Like Tarik, I used to sit in the tea garden beside the Beyazit mosque and watch Friday afternoon riots.

The historical framework in which the story of Jesus the Infidel takes place is also accurate. The sad role of the missionaries, the story of the ancient churches, the massacres of 1843-46, 1895 and 1914-15 are all well documented. I drew from Bob Blinco's disturbing book *Ethnic Issues and the Church*, Martin van Bruinessen's *Agha, Sheikh and State* and the *Annual Reports of the American Board of Commissioners* to help me sketch the past.

The social framework in which this story takes place also reflects reality. I have drawn from the autobiographies of three Christians who grew up in Anatolia to help me paint authentic cameos of daily life, as well as give accurate descriptions of the various ethnic groups and of the districts of Amîd they once occupied. The books of Kirkor Ceyhan (*Seferberlik Türküleriyle Büyüdüm*), Mıgırdıç Magosyan (*Biletimiz İstanbul'a Kesildi; Söyle Margos, Nerelisin; Gâvur Mahallesi*) and Hagop Mintzuri (*Armidan Fırat'in Öte Yanı*) are all published by Aras Yayıncılık (Aras Publishing, Istanbul) and do justice to its claim to be a "window into Armenian culture". Sadly none of these books have, as yet, been translated into English. Chapters four, five, nine, thirteen, sixteen, twenty and twenty-five are, essentially, a compendium of the experiences of these men, and of Magosyan in particular. Jesus and Tarik's visit to Mardin is loosely based on an event described in Magosyan's *Gâvur Mahallesi*.

Other scenes reflect my own experiences. I learned my first Kurdish words and phrases in Bezal during a series of extended visits there in the 1980s. It was there that I first observed a travelling dentist administering his crude craft on the hapless villagers; it was a mesmerizing performance, and I looked on with indecent fascination. I was in Bezal when a neighbouring tribe attacked. What tension, what fear, what sense of adventure, what adrenaline, surged through me as the AK47s, that favourite weapon of guerrillas the world over, popped around us. The mountains and the cliff magnified and multiplied the erratic bursts. I'll be forever grateful for the palpable anxiety the villagers of Bezal had for my safety; I was their guest of honour and if anything horrible happened to me they would lose face. Four men lost their lives in that exchange. Nor will I forget the torturous excitement and the frantic loading and unloading in the dead of a moonless night prompted by the arrival of a convoy of donkeys. The methods used by those called to the hazardous occupation of smuggling across the Turkish, Iraqi, Iranian, and Syrian borders are accurately described.

"The General" stands for the succession of military huntas and army-supported regimes that have held political power in Turkey since the modern republic rose from the ashes of the Ottoman Empire in 1923 until the 1990s. Thankfully, things have changed since then; the country is now a candidate for membership into the European Union.

Tarik and his father are figments of the imagination, literary devices used to tell an essentially true tale. Numerous suggestions by Seán Virgo, the meticulous editor Thistledown Press assigned me, has, I trust, helped turn an interesting manuscript into literature.

And Jesus? How real is he? His life-story is woven together from strands I picked up from Syriac, Chaldean and Kurdish friends. As for his name? Well, it isn't just that that happens to be a fairly common name among both the Muslim and the Christian tribes of the Middle East, but also because he has a message for those with ears to hear and eyes to see.

— *Pierre Piccard*

Originally from Hamilton, Ontario, Pierre Piccard has spend a lifetime coming to know the Middle East intimately through his educational missionary work. He has studied at Prairie Bible College, the Universities of Jordan, Istanbul, Syracuse, and South Africa, speaks Arabic and Turkish and has degrees in Theology and Social Science. He teaches Theology, Cross-Cultural Communication and History of Christian/Muslim Relations at a theological institute in the region. *The Infidel* Piccard's first novel.